DEATH AND THE I CHING

DEATH
AND THE
I CHING

a mystery novel by
Lulla Rosenfeld

Clarkson N. Potter, Inc./Publishers

DISTRIBUTED BY CROWN PUBLISHERS, INC., NEW YORK

To PEARL,

who loves all riddles

Published simultaneously in Canada by General Publishing Company Limited
Library of Congress Cataloging in Publication Data
Rosenfeld, Lulla.
Death and the I Ching.
I. Title.
PZ4.R7256De [PS3568.0815] 813'.54 79-27518
ISBN: 0-517-540290
Design by Deborah B. Kerner
10 9 8 7 6 5 4 3 2 1
First Edition

*If a person consulting the oracle
is not in touch with tao
he does not receive an intelligible answer,
since it would be of no avail.*

—THE I CHING

DEATH AND THE I CHING

Prologue

"Can you really work it, Keith?" Bacchus wanted to know. "Don't you need yarrow stalks and incense and all the rest of it?"

"It would probably be better with yarrow," Keith Tilden admitted. "There's a whole ritual actually. The three obeisances, and the facing north and the business with the divining sticks. But none of it really matters except to get you into the right state of mind, the right inner attitude. If you have that, you can use any system." He looked around at the others and smiled. "Well, we can't get yarrow at this hour," he pointed out. "So shall we go ahead with the coins?" And without waiting for an answer, he laid his three pennies out on the table.

"Fun!" Letty Tilden said. She came around to look over his shoulder. "You throw the coins, is that it? And then we get the answer—here?" She touched the edge of the magic book with a cautious fingertip.

"Try it and see."

"But the answer—will it be true?" Letty was balanced between doubt and fascination. "Really, really true, Keith?" she persisted. "Always?"

"Oh, yes!" he answered coolly. "The answer will be really true—always."

This produced a ripple of amusement, but all the same everyone came closer. Midge, frankly intrigued, came up to the table to watch. Arnaboldi and Dr. Jackman came up behind her. Bacchus, too, drew nearer by a step. Even Bettina, seated with Keith on the little bench, moved toward him with small wriggling movements. The whole little group drew in, magnetized by the three coins, the magic book and the youthful bearded magician. Only Kenneth Stramm remained outside the circle, resisting the pull.

"Now, let's get something really good" Bill Bacchus suggested. Host and genial conspirator, he dominated the proceedings by the sheer mass of his physical presence. "It ought to be something, you know—oh, tremendously interesting and important."

"Peace?" Bettina whispered.

"The assassination?"

"Life on other planets?"

Letty broke in, bored. "Nobody cares about all that!" she declared. "There's only one thing in all the universe that matters now. Surely you know what it is!" Smiling and incredulous, she waited for them to see it.

"By God!" Arnaboldi cried, and struck his forehead with his palm. "She's right!"

"The play!" Midge cried.

"By God, the play!" Dr. Jackman echoed.

Excited laughter broke out.

"But do we dare?" Bacchus said. "Aren't you terrified, Letty? To know—to really *know?*"

"Oh, for once in our lives!" And turning to Keith with a reckless laugh, she said, "Fate be damned. Do we have a hit or don't we?"

Keith gathered up the three coins with a sweep of his hand.

"Seven, seven, come eleven!" Dr. Jackman shouted.

Midge covered her face. "Don't do it!" she begged.

Bacchus said, "We started this. Let's have it, Keith. Good or bad."

Six times Keith threw his coins out on the table, pronouncing each time some presumably Chinese formula. Bettina bent over

2

the little ivory notebook, her hair a silken curtain parting on a triangle of lovely white face. With each throw of the coins she drew mystic lines with a tiny ivory pencil. After the sixth throw, she laid notebook and pencil aside and consulted a chart at the back of the book. "Oh, Keith!" she murmured happily. "They've got Possession in Great Measure."

"Is that good?" someone asked with a suppressed giggle.

"Shhhh!"

An expectant silence.

Bettina turned pages, found her place and in her flat uninflected little voice read aloud from the book. "'Possession in Great Measure accords with the time. The time is favorable. Strength is within, clarity without. Power is expressing itself in a graceful and controlled way. This brings supreme success and wealth.'"

A storm of approval broke out.

"Bravo! Bravo, Bettina!" Arnaboldi was up on his feet. "Letty—Bill!" he called gaily. "We are a smash!"

"Supreme success!" Letty repeated. "Read it again, you angel! The part where it says supreme success!"

"And wealth," Bacchus reminded her. "Don't forget it said wealth!"

"How did it go?" Letty was trying to remember. "There was something about power—power expressing itself?"

"With grace!" Arnaboldi recalled excitedly. "Power and grace. Fantastic."

"What I can't get over," said Midge, "is the way it *answered.*"

"Oh, it was an absolute answer," Arnaboldi declared.

"It was absolute drivel" came a drawling voice outside the circle.

The excited chatter and laughter died down.

"Well, I'm sorry. I really am," Kenneth Stramm said with a nervous laugh. "But supreme success is really a bit thick. I mean this play—it's terribly deep and obscure, terribly Beckett—but it's just a rather pretentious imitation. We all know that, I hope." He looked around the circle of disapproving faces. "Have I said something wrong?" he inquired. "I always do."

3

"Oh, not at all," Bacchus replied with heavy irony.

"I mean, let's play Spin the Bottle," Stramm said. "Let's play Post Office. Those were nice games too. At least you got to kiss the girls."

"But we were having fun, Kenneth!" Letty broke in, annoyed. "Why must you spoil it? We know it's just a game."

"Not to me," Bacchus declared roundly. "I've been promised supreme success, and I won't take anything less."

"You must admit," Dr. Jackman told Stramm playfully, "that the mystic response, if nothing else, was surprisingly germane."

Stramm turned his admiring gaze on the doctor. "Now I find that really fascinating!" he exclaimed. "I must admit I wouldn't have imagined that a doctor, a scientific man, would put his faith in this kind of thing."

The doctor reddened and said it was not a question of faith.

"But your view as a doctor—as a scientific man—"

"All right, Kenneth!" Letty cut in, "Knock it off, can't you? Let up on it."

"But don't you find it interesting that Dr. Jackman—everyone knows he's a scientific man—"

"Let it go," Letty repeated. "Let up on it. Can't you, for God's sake, ever let up on it?" Her voice went up with an ugly repressed violence.

"But all I said was that Dr. Jackman—"

Letty was looking around the room distractedly. "Is this the way it's going to be?" she demanded. "Always this? For the rest of my life? Forever?"

"Oh, it needn't be forever, Letty!" Stramm said with a smile. He had turned rather white. "People can always back out of things. Even at the last moment."

"Damned good idea!" Letty said shortly.

After some silence Midge remarked that it was growing late. Letty agreed.

At this moment, with a confused feeling of departures in the offing, Kenneth Stramm declared loudly that he had a question for Keith's magic book. "I want to ask if it's true what they say

4

about Chinese girls!" He laughed wildly. "I'm in love with a beautiful Chinese lady, and I want to know if the rumors—if the rumors—"

"We've had enough magic for one night," Bacchus broke in fretfully. "Why don't we forget all this and have some fresh drinks. Letty! It's absurd to break things up this early. Midge, come, help me fix the drinks."

"Of course!" Arnaboldi seconded him with enthusiasm. "We will not break up Bill's wonderful party. We will have a drink instead: a drink to Letty and Kenneth! To the happy occasion! Right, Kenneth?" He threw a comradely arm over Stramm's shoulder. Stramm knocked it away.

"How about it, Keith?" he called. "I want an answer from the magic book."

"You won't get an answer to that," Keith told him.

"Why not? You'll get *some* answer if you toss those coins."

"But you must approach the oracle with reverence, Kenneth," Bettina pleaded beautifully. "The question must come from the *highest* part of your being, not from the—"

"How about a horse?" Kenneth interrupted, laughing. "I've got a filly in the third at Aqueduct—" He looked around. "Won't the horse do either? Not reverent enough? Maybe the book will answer this one. How do Keith and Bettina reconcile all this magic with the ideas of the New Left and the counterculture?"

"Oh, if he's beginning on the New Left and the counterculture we may as well give up," Midge exclaimed in an audible undertone.

"It's a good question!" Stramm insisted. "Do Keith and Bettina really want to change society by means of astrology, pot, group sex, and witchcraft?"

Bettina turned pink. Keith said nothing.

"Kenneth, old boy!" Bacchus addressed him rather pityingly. "Do you really have to go on with this?"

"But I want the answer," Stramm persisted, laughing.

"Oh, go ahead and do it, Keith!" Midge broke in hysterically. "We'll be here all night if you don't!"

5

Bettina unexpectedly spoke up and said the question was valid.

Keith shrugged and took up the coins again. Bettina tore away the top page of the little ivory notebook, crumpled it, threw it into the fireplace and waited, ivory pencil poised.

In the pause that followed a great mild gust of wind came blowing in at the open window. As it died down, a grandfather clock somewhere in the recesses of the house slowly and ponderously struck the hour.

"Oh, didn't all this happen once before?" Midge cried strangely.

"But when?" Letty mused.

The others laughed uneasily. For a curious moment the objects around them lost their reality; they were all adrift in the endless colorless well of Time. "One! Two!" said the grandfather clock. The hour was going. The night was going. And the future, too—all that lay before them and could still so easily be changed—all that too was flowing, flowing back forever, into the immutable, unchanging past.

The chimes lingered on the air and died. The spell lifted. They were together once again, a little dazed to find they were fixed at the same point.

Still, in that odd timeless interval, something had shifted, and they were aware of a choice. A word, a jest, and all these old antagonists might yet clasp hands tonight. There was still time for a truce, time for folly and anger and pain to fall away like the cruel illusions they were.

The moment slipped past. The word remained unuttered.

"What is your question?" Keith Tilden impassively asked.

Stupidly—against his own judgment, against his own deepest wish—Kenneth Stramm repeated it.

Letty Tilden shrugged. Keith Tilden swept up the three coins and threw them out on the table.

But the answer, when it came, seemed to make no sense at all.

Standstill

Heaven and earth moving apart—
the image of Standstill.
Disorder and confusion prevail.

It was close to five in the morning when Nick Armisen came
back to the gray brick house on Washington Street. Faint streaks
of pink were showing in the east, and all the way along the river
front the rooftops made a dark irregular outline against the sky. A
chilly little wind was blowing. There wasn't a soul on the street
but himself.

The long night had left a garrulous echo in his head, and a
blurred recollection of many faces and many rooms. Now,
hands dug into the pockets of his trench coat, he stood gazing up
at the dark housefront. No life stirred behind those silent upper

windows. Bacchus's party was over, his great front door shut up tight.

Nick went down three steps into an areaway, let himself in with his key and walked past the automatic elevator in the hall. He was thinking, with an acute sense of loss, of the big stone sculpture in the court behind his studio. Known to the art world as *Empyrean*, it was one of the best things he had ever done, and he had sold it that night to a couple from Cleveland. They were pleasant young people, rich enough to have bought flashier work by one of the younger men. It was rather nice of them to want a Nicholas Armisen on their Shaker Heights lawn. But in a few days the piece would be shipped out. Gone. As he unlocked his studio door, Nick decided he was not too tired to spend a quarter of an hour in the sculpture court looking at what he was soon to lose.

He was all the more surprised as he walked in, to find the room flooded by a strong shaft of artificial light coming through the glass doors leading out into the court. Someone had apparently come down while he was gone and turned on the illumination out there. But why? He was certain he had not left the lights on himself.

He started across the room toward the switch that controlled the court but stopped abruptly halfway. This time he remained motionless, looking out. He was trying to understand what he saw.

The sculpture, of a rough dark stone, rose only five feet above its pedestal and was remarkable in that it suggested illimitable heights. It dominated everything else in the court. And bathed in the powerful electric illumination, Kenneth Stramm was climbing over the top of it. Perched thus in the air, he peered in through the glass doors, grinning slyly at Nick's surprise.

"Hello, Kenneth!" Nick heard himself say in a tone of thin amazement.

A great false sense of understanding swept over him. In spite of the darkened windows on the street, the party upstairs was *not* over. On the contrary, it was in full swing, with some wild game in progress down here in the court.

A strangely silent game. As Nick grinned back at the man outside, an unpleasant warmth broke out over his body. The floor under his feet seemed suddenly to dip. He backed away wildly, clattering into a chair. He shouted something too but did not make out his own words through the roaring in his ears.

The moment of panic subsided, leaving him undamaged but with a heart going extremely hard. Kenneth Stramm was still peering in through the glass doors. He was dead, of course. One side of his head was smashed all to hell. Nick could see that even from here.

Before he had fully gotten back his breath, Nick was assessing the situation. Uppermost in his mind was the cool recognition that he himself was in an extremely unpleasant and possibly dangerous fix. Under this he was noting, just as coolly, that something about the spectacle in the court was wrong. Framed by the glass doors, theatrically lit by expensive floodlights, it looked somehow *staged*. But this was only a fleeting impression, and Nick dismissed it as irrelevant. In some way beyond his understanding, a dead man had been slung across the top of his sculpture. His next move was clear. He had to call the police.

It was, however, a more familiar number that his unsteady hand found on the telephone dial. And in the unaccustomed quiet, he could actually hear the ringing of the phone in the room two storys over his head. After two rings the phone was picked up on the other end. A low, cold, tired voice said, "Yes." Just the one word.

"Bill?" Nick gripped the phone hard. "Is that you, Bill?"

Again that low, cold "Yes."

"Bill, it's Nick. Nick Armisen."

"Yes, Nick," came the calm response. "What's up? Where are you?"

"I'm down here in the studio. Something totally grotesque has happened here, Bill. You've got to come down right away. We've got to call the police."

"The police? Why?"

Nick told him.

"Dead, you say? Dead? *Stramm?* But he was just *here!* He was

9

just—" The crazy babble of words abruptly stopped. When Bacchus spoke again, it was with sharp authority. "Don't do anything! Not yet! I'll be down in three minutes."

The connection was broken.

After a moment Nick walked quietly out into the court.

It was shadowy and damp and still out there. Only a few faint birdcalls and the muffled early traffic on West Street broke the quiet. The big childish face against the stone was neither a dream nor a waking apparition. It was just a cold, gray reality in the cold, gray light.

Walking around to the back of the sculpture, Nick saw why the body had not slipped off but hung there in that curious scarecrow fashion. A great jagged V-shaped cleft, here, divided the stone almost to its base. Nick remembered how beautiful he had once thought that bold division of the stone. It was not beautiful now. The dead man's left arm, halfway to the elbow, was violently thrust into this granite chasm. The force of the thrust had broken the arm, ripping the shirt and jacket sleeve to the shoulder. The whole body hung sideways from the broken arm with the heels, lifeless as those of a puppet, dangling above the ground.

Not far from these terrible dead feet a white object was fluttering in the wind. Nick stopped and picked it up: a small ivory notebook or memorandum pad with tear-away pages and a little ivory pencil on a gold chain. Engraved on the ivory was the name "Lorette Harris Tilden." An odd little six-line hieroglyphic had been drawn on the top page.

Nick turned the notebook over in his hand, hesitated, and dropped it into his pocket.

Walking back across the grass, he found himself treading on coins. Keys. A fountain pen. A billfold. From what indifferent heaven this rain of terrible prosaic objects? Instinctively he glanced up to where the topmost windows of the house yawned dark over the court. "That's how it happened," he muttered aloud. "He fell."

He went back into the studio, crossed the floor and opened the door just as the automatic elevator in the hall came down.

Bacchus came out of the elevator and, after him, Keith Tilden.

"Where is he? Where is Stramm?" Bacchus immediately demanded. He was coming down the hall as fast as his bulk would allow and in his dark dressing gown with its high Mao neck, he looked more than ever like some enormous comic priest. But the authentic forbidding look of tragedy was etched into every line of the great Buddha-face, and terrible fear had bleached the cheeks.

"Hold it!" Nick stopped both men in the doorway and took a deep breath. "He must have fallen out of the window. It's the only way it could have happened. He's caught, you see. He's caught in the big sculpture out there."

"I don't understand," Bacchus rapped out. "Are you saying Kenneth fell out of a window onto your sculpture?"

"He's jammed down *into* the sculpture."

At that Keith Tilden shouldered past him into the room and stood motionless, looking through the glass doors. Bacchus slowly followed. It had grown lighter in these last minutes, and both men got the full shock of that frightful spectacle in the court. Bacchus blurted out, "Ah, my Christ!" His face puckered into a baby's mask of grief, tears spurted from his eyes, a violent shudder passed through him, and he fell onto his knees. Nick and Keith had to help him up and get him into a chair. He had collapsed so utterly that even Keith Tilden turned away with a quiver of emotion.

"Why did it have to happen? Why?" Bacchus demanded, sobbing. "I wanted everyone to be together. I wanted everyone to be happy!" Nick, thoroughly unnerved, brought him some whiskey in a tumbler. He took this with both hands, like a child,

11

gasped as he got it down, grew calmer and at last said, quietly and hopelessly, "This is how it ends."

He nodded in a dazed way when Nick mentioned police, but a moment later lifted himself out of the chair and ordered him to wait. Tottering across the room, he caught at Nick's arm and began pleading for time. "They'll want to know things, Nick," he explained. "They'll ask me things—and I'm mixed up. I've got to remember. I've got to put it all together—" He continued to hang on to Nick's arm. For Nick this was almost harder than anything else.

"What happened?" he asked Keith through his teeth.

Keith said slowly, "I don't know. Bettina and I left early. I've been back less than an hour."

"Give me time!" Bacchus gasped. He shut his eyes, concentrating every ounce of his strength. After a moment of this he began talking in a low monotone. "Yes! Arnaboldi came first, a little past eleven. Then the others, all of them together. Letty, Kenneth, Midge Jackman and her husband all came together from the broadcasting studio. That's why the party started so late—because Letty was on television tonight."

He tightened his grip convulsively on Nick's arm. "They all got here. The model for the second act set was up in my studio. Everybody wanted to see it. We took the elevator up to the top floor. How long were we there, Keith? Ten minutes?"

"Less."

"Even less. We looked at the model and came down again. I had prepared a little buffet in the living room. We had some drinks. Keith and Bettina left. After that a sort of discussion took place." Bacchus slowed down here as though he didn't remember this part too well. "A sort of—general discussion. And then—yes! We split up! That's it!" He let go of Nick's arm and his voice shot up to normal volume. "We split up," he repeated. "Midge and I went into the bar to fix some fresh drinks for people. Everyone else remained in the living room. Now wait!" Bacchus lifted his hand for silence. "At a certain point Kenneth Stramm walked out of the living room. He never came back." Again that commanding gesture. "I found that out later, of course. At the time I could not be aware of Kenneth's movements, since I was in the bar with Midge Jackman."

He began walking up and down. He was speaking now with his usual somewhat mechanical precision and Nick saw that within the limits of the situation he would soon be capable even of wit. It was a demonstration of iron control, of a mask assumed over a lifetime, and in the end, admirable as character itself.

"Now you must understand," he continued didactically, "that none of us had the faintest idea anything was wrong. Those in the living room assumed that Kenneth had simply joined Midge and myself in the bar. We just as naturally assumed he was still with the others in the living room. It was only later, when the party broke up—"

"That you realized he was missing?"

"But we didn't realize anything." Bacchus stared at him. "We realized nothing at all. We simply thought he had gone off for some reason. You know how erratic he was. Everyone forgot it and went home."

"And all the time—?"

Bacchus nodded with infinite regret. "He must have gone back upstairs at some point. Somehow, fooling with the window up there— As you know, it opens outward. The handles have a way of sticking and then *turning*—"

Nick was trying to see it. The man alone in the big room on the top floor. A false movement at the window. A plunge. An unheard cry. Yes, it could have happened that way. Yet, somehow, the whole thing didn't hang together. "When were you all playing with the I Ching?" he asked.

Neither of them answered. Nick had the curious impression that they were both *listening* to something. Two men at sea who had felt the unmistakable vibration of a depth bomb might listen with just that carefully attentive expression. Bacchus shook it off as a dog shakes off water. "We *were* doing that, Nick," he said with a brilliant smile, "but however did you know it?"

Nick held out the ivory-backed notebook with its little drawing on the top page. "It *is* an I Ching symbol, isn't it?" he asked curiously. Both men seemed to have fallen into a peculiar

13

reverie. "I found it in the grass out there," Nick explained. "Apparently it belongs to Letty, so I thought it might be best to—"

Bacchus gave an approving grunt. "No reason the police should have it. By the way, we ought to call them. We've waited rather long to do that."

The clock stood at six minutes past five. "Before I call," Nick said. "Somebody came down last night and turned on the floodlights in the court. Was there some reason for that?"

Bacchus looked blank. "Nobody was down here, Nick. You must have left them on yourself."

Nick, already occupied with a larger problem, let it go. They were waiting for him to make the call, yet he lingered, hesitant and uneasy. "I don't suppose"—he was trying to frame this carefully—"I don't suppose there's any way we could leave Letty out of this."

Bacchus shook his head. "No way at all."

"Why not?" Keith demanded. "Why do we have to say she was here?"

"It won't do, Keith," Bacchus said. "She and Kenneth left the broadcasting studio together. Too many people saw them. Too many people know they were to have been married today. It won't do."

A silence followed.

"I suppose this may be complicated," Nick said.

Nobody contradicted him.

"Well," he said at last, "I'd better make the call."

He was halfway to the phone when he wheeled around again, with a definite shock.

Keith Tilden's face, as usual, was entirely without expression. He had just switched off the floodlights in the court.

Biting Through

The situation bodes ill
but favors the process of the law.
The theme of this hexagram
is a criminal lawsuit.

In the next hour a number of things happened. A couple of patrolmen drove up in a prowl car and took down the facts. An ambulance pulled up soon after. This was followed by a special equipment truck with a crew of four men, all of them now out in the court, trying to pry Kenneth Stramm out of the sculpture. A small crowd had collected across the street to watch the proceedings. And a news photographer had climbed a back fence with his camera, been punched in the lip by Keith Tilden, and got away with his picture.

Bacchus had told his story first to Nick and then to the

15

patrolmen. He was now going through it a third time for two men from Manhattan South Homicide, a Lieutenant Goodine and a sergeant called Shellman. Both of them heard him out without comment, and then asked to see the rest of the house. Everyone crowded silently into the automatic elevator and rode up to the parlor floor, where Bacchus led the party into his study.

This was a room lined with books with a large workmanlike desk at one end, and a well-stocked bar at the other. It was here, Bacchus said, that he and Mrs. Jackman had spent the last hour of the party.

"We came in here to get fresh drinks for the others," he explained. "We got to talking and more or less forgot about the drinks."

"Can happen," Goodine agreed with a smile. He was a tall fair-haired man, finely built and with a surprising quality of physical grace. He was wearing a light topcoat of some hard-looking tweed. The other man, dark and of medium height, stood back against the books and let Goodine do the talking. Both men wore decent inexpensive clothes and had pleasant courteous manners.

"Let me see," Goodine resumed. "You and Mrs. Jackman came in here leaving Mr. Stramm with the others?"

"Exactly."

"Who stayed with him in the other room?"

Bacchus went through the names. Leopold Arnaboldi. Dr. Ralph Jackman. Mrs. Lorette Tilden. That was all. Keith Tilden and Miss Hodges, Bacchus said, had left the house before he and Mrs. Jackman went into the bar.

Goodine jotted the names in a notebook, using the stub of a pencil. He took a good deal of time over this and afterward continued to study the list. "This Lorette Tilden," he inquired. "Would that be Lorette *Harris* Tilden?"

Bacchus replied, "Lorette Harris, for a good many years now, has been Mrs. Tilden's professional name."

Goodine shut up his book and asked to see the living room.

16

This was situated just across the hall. It was a large, formal room with fashionable cocoa-colored walls, a fireplace, and a great deal of wood paneling. Here, Bacchus said, they had all discovered that Stramm was missing.

"It was getting late. Mrs. Jackman and I came back to the others. Everyone asked us where Stramm was. They had assumed he was with us in the bar."

"Mmm—yes." Goodine was looking around the room. "I suppose some attempt was made to locate him?"

"Oh, yes. We all called out, of course, as one does. I went upstairs and looked into both bedrooms. I even climbed halfway to the top floor and called out. Several times. There was no answer, so I came down again. We were all extremely puzzled, but nobody so much as dreamed—"

"Yes, we have that." Goodine looked a little bored with it. He turned to Keith. "You and this young lady left early. About what time was that, would you say?"

"After two." Keith's reply was so slurred and low that Goodine had to ask him to repeat it.

"Where did you go when you left here?"

"Two Dakotas."

"What's that?" Goodine's voice turned sharp.

"It's a restaurant," the other man told him. "East Village hangout."

"I see." Goodine was looking Keith over a second time. Nick's pulses jumped. He had been worried about Keith from the start. The flowered shirt opening on the hairy muscular torso, the Che Guevara beard, the crucified eyes—all this could only take these men back to the Chicago riots, a memory that still rankled.

"How long were you in this restaurant?"

"'Til it closed." He shrugged, his face surly.

"Where did you go afterward?"

"Bettina took a cab back to Riverdale. I came home."

"What time was that?"

"Four, maybe."

"Did you know what had happened here?"

17

A pause. Then, very low and deliberate, "How the —— would I know what happened here?"

Another pause.

"Take it easy, son," Goodine advised in a level voice.

Very low: *"Then don't crowd me!"*

Goodine looked at the other man and some signal passed between them. The sergeant stepped forward. Nick, watching him, knew he had disliked this man from the beginning.

"You go to college?" he asked Keith.

"Is that important?"

"We'll be the judge of that. You just answer."

"No, I don't go to college."

"How come?"

No answer.

"Rather go to Vietnam?" With a noiseless laugh.

No answer.

"You're Mrs. Tilden's son, right?"

"I'm her son."

"How come you're living here instead of at home?"

"I'm twenty years old. There's no law I have to live with my mother."

"No, there's no law." The sergeant looked him up and down. "Did you like this Kenneth Stramm?"

"He was okay."

"Sure he was." The sergeant smiled. "You don't seem very sorry he's dead."

"Just a moment!" Bacchus was white to his lips. "If Mr. Tilden is to be grilled here, I am calling in Harold Lasher." He had named a leading attorney, and the two men could not have liked him for it.

"He can refuse to answer," Goodine pointed out.

"We are perfectly willing to answer!" Bacchus snapped. "We are not willing to be baited."

"Quite right." Another signal. The sergeant fell back, no pleasant light in his eye.

An exchange followed with Nick.

18

"You discovered the body?" the sergeant asked.

"Yes. I got home about five o'clock and saw something through the glass door that looked wrong."

"Would you mind giving us an idea of how you spent the evening, Mr. Armisen?" Smoothly, "Just as part of the general picture."

Nick didn't like it, but it was best to comply. He went through the events of his own night quickly. The Cleveland couple at seven that evening. The hour in the sculpture court while they looked over *Empyrean* and made arrangements for its purchase. The dinner afterward with the Cleveland couple at an Italian restaurant on MacDougal Street. The departure of the Cleveland couple for the airport and Cleveland. The loft party thrown by his friend, George Maxfield. The last hour at an all-night cafeteria on the east side. The long walk home across town, and the discovery of the body in the court.

Goodine made one or two notes but asked no questions. Nick, outwardly cool, was hoping he had not made a bad mistake. He had deliberately omitted one fact. Though the omission troubled him, he told himself there was nothing else he could have done.

They left the living room and followed Bacchus up the stair.

Two large bedrooms took up most of the second-floor space, with a linen closet and an extra bath in the hall. The guest room, occupied by Keith Tilden, had windows on the street. The master bedroom, occupied by Bacchus, had a window on the court, but since this was sealed by an air conditioner, it had no importance.

Halfway up the last flight of stairs, Goodine turned once again to Bacchus. "What about the lights last night?" he inquired pleasantly. "The lights up there, I mean. Were they on?" He indicated the top-floor landing above them.

"You mean when I came up looking for—for Stramm?" Bacchus seemed to be floundering a little.

"You were here on the stairs, Mr. Bacchus. About where we are standing now, I imagine. Was it dark up there, or were the lights on?"

19

After a slight pause Bacchus said, "The lights were on."

"You did not go up and turn them off?"

"No, I did not. As I told you, I called out two or three times. When nobody answered, I came down again."

"There are no lights up there now," Goodine pointed out.

Bacchus said quietly, "There's a switch at the foot of the stairs. I turned them out as I came down."

That was all. They left the second floor and proceeded on up to the top.

Here, after a cursory look at a makeshift kitchen and bath, they halted briefly at a small workroom used these past weeks by Keith Tilden. Unfinished pieces of wire and aluminum sculpture, a broken easel, sculptor's tools on a worktable, magazines, clothing, even several musical instruments—all in hopeless disorder. The detectives glanced in without interest, and then asked Bacchus to take them into the main studio.

Entering this room, Nick was immediately conscious of something wrong. Something up here was either missing or displaced. Once again Nick had a feeling things had been *arranged* in some way. But the impression, again, was fleeting. He quickly forgot it.

Nick had always thought this room the finest in the house. Bacchus did his real work in a warehouse uptown. This was a showplace. Less formal than the living room downstairs, it had far more real magnificence. Finely proportioned for its size, the room ran the length of the building from front to back, with windows at both ends. Bacchus had furnished it with wonderful massive pieces, the wood floors glowed and gleamed, and on either side of a vast fireplace, priceless paintings lined the whitewashed walls. Three of Bacchus's cool geometric canvases were on view here—Bacchus doubled as a painter and liked to be thought of as such. There were also a number of things done by his friends, among them a very good still life by Nick himself.

The miniature stage set was centrally displayed on a special table. Complete with turntables, and accurate to the thirty-secondth of an inch, it represented with a most fascinating reality a tiny room in a broken-down palace. Hangings of deep red velvet fell in tatters over the tall miniature windows; strips of threadbare carpet had been tacked along the floor; and on a raised dais, a tiny broken throne leaned crazily on three legs.

Even these hardened detectives showed some surprise at this extraordinary object.

"Is this the model of the stage set you were speaking about?" A hint of real respect had come into Goodine's voice.

"Yes, I completed it a few days ago. It's the second act of a play called *The Masquers*. We're going into rehearsal next month."

Nick was afraid Bacchus was going to offer him tickets. But Goodine's interest in the model had faded. He had eyes only for the window over the court. Very hard eyes they were, too.

Originally, Nick knew, the window had opened outward onto a small balcony. But Bacchus had recently converted his ground floor into a studio. Nick was the first tenant to occupy this space, and Bacchus had made certain alterations for him. The rear wall of Nick's ground-floor apartment had been built out so that a skylight could be installed. And since the projecting balcony on the top floor cut off some of the light from the sculpture court, Bacchus had had the balcony removed. Under pressure in his own work, he had put off replacing the window itself, and for the past week it had opened, with its dangerously low sill, onto empty space.

It was unquestionably by way of this window that Kenneth Stramm had met his death; it looked directly over that fatal sculpture in the court below.

Goodine looked narrowly at the metal handles, but was careful not to touch them. "So you think Mr. Stramm came up here, tried to push this window open and accidentally fell out?"

"I can't think of any other way it could have happened," Bacchus replied.

"Why would he come up here at all?"

"He might perhaps have left something, forgotten something. We were all up here for a little while."

21

"You think he came back to get something?"

"It's possible."

"And opened the window?" Goodine looked dubious.

"I can't say about that. It was a warm night, and it does get close up here."

Goodine nodded absently. Suddenly he leaned out as far as possible, and then drew in his head again.

"That would do it," he remarked to the sergeant. "He fell feet first, you see, with both his arms *down*." He illustrated with his own arms. "By a stroke of bad luck, his hand and part of the arm drove into that crack in the statue, or sculpture, or whatever it is, down there. Force of the fall drove the arm in quite a way."

"Freak thing," the sergeant commented.

"Remarkable. At the same time, his head hit the top of the stone. As soon as that happened, he was out. According to the coroner, the axis bone was broken. That would make it instantaneous. The body flipped over, but hung there because of the trapped arm."

"He had bad luck all right," the sergeant said. "If not for that statue thing down there he would maybe have gotten off with just a few broken bones. It's not that much of a fall."

"Yes. Bad luck."

They conferred about something in low tones, and Goodine turned again. Nick got the impression that something had now been settled.

"Did anyone leave the living room last night?" he asked Bacchus. "Aside from Mr. Stramm, I mean?"

"Well, there's no way I can be sure of that," Bacchus pointed out.

"Well, you do see, Mr. Bacchus—" Goodine's manner had become much more friendly. "You do see the man would never have fallen as he did—*facing* the house—if he had pitched out *forward*."

Bacchus stared at him. His face and bald head were slowly turning a dark constricted red. "I don't understand," he said in a forced voice.

"It's easy enough to see, Mr. Bacchus. From the position he's

22

in now, he could only have been standing with his *back* to the window when he fell."

"But in that case—!" Nick suddenly stopped short.

"Exactly!" Goodine gave him an approving nod. "If you'll step over to the window, Mr. Armisen, you'll see what I mean."

Nick stayed where he was. His heart was hammering steadily in his chest. There was no need to go to the window. One had only to visualize Stramm's body plunging down backward, and one saw at once that the lieutenant was quite correct.

Attraction

The attraction is present,
but those involved
are not yet aware of it.

"Nicholas Armisen?"

The newsmen closed in as soon as he opened the taxi door. One of them aimed a camera at him. A flash went off.

There were several of them, all walking with him toward the hotel entrance, the one with the camera dancing lightly and expertly backward.

"Have you anything to say about the Stramm case, Mr. Armisen?"

"There is no case," Nick said. "It was an accident."

"Do you know why Mrs. Tilden was not at the funeral yesterday?"

"Do you know if Mrs. Tilden will open next month in *The Masquers?*"

"No, I don't." Nick stopped. Another flash went off. "Look here, you men," he broke out irritably. "Haven't you anything better to do than hang around down here?"

"We think this is news, Mr. Armisen," one of them answered.

Nick shouldered past him and pushed through the heavy glass revolving door. He thought the reporters would follow, but they remained outside, laughing and talking among themselves. The doorman told Nick the man with the camera had offered him five dollars to pass him into the elevator.

After some trouble with his name on the intercom, Nick was directed to a suite on the third floor. Midge opened the door, every golden hair in place, her diminutive figure impeccably tailored in pale gray. "Nick! My God!" she said. "How absolutely marvelous to see you."

"I didn't think you were going to let me up," Nick said. "Did you think I was a reporter?"

"Don't mention the word!" She shuddered. "Are they still down there?"

"They are, damn them. They got my picture, too!"

"Well, now you know what we've been through."

The hall was wide, dimly lit and heavily carpeted. A murmur of talk came from beyond an archway, and then Letty's voice, high and hysterical: "I don't care about that—just *give* it to me!"

"Oh, Lord!" Midge breathed, frowning.

Nick hoped he had not come at the wrong time.

Midge shook her head, listening. "It's just that she's asking for liquor," she explained, looking worried, "and Ralph has her on tranquilizers."

"Is she up to seeing people?"

"That's all we've had for three days," Midge told him wearily. "They come in droves. Some of them never go!"

Nick followed her through the archway into a large room with the afternoon sun slanting in through many windows. On a

Steinway grand, the square, ugly, famous face of John Keith Tilden scowled out of a chrome frame. A silver coffee service and a large tray of sandwiches had been laid out on a table.

Bacchus gave him a calm "Hello there, Nick." Keith Tilden, not a believer in the amenities, offered no greeting at all. A short man with a toothbrush moustache and large doggy eyes transferred a sandwich to his left hand and shook hands with Nick with his right. Nick placed him after a while as Midge Jackman's husband, recalling also that he was a doctor and had recently been in the papers for something vaguely unethical.

Letty had gotten her drink and was seated with it on the couch. She was wearing a dark red robe of some kind of shot silk; it was wrinkled and one of the buttons hung by a thread. She gazed at Nick with eyes that were black lifeless smudges in a coarse, swollen face. She had put on fifteen pounds since Nick had seen her last and looked at least that many years older. The floor beneath her feet was littered with open newspapers.

"It's Nick, dear!" Midge said. "Nick Armisen!"

"I see who it is," Letty answered.

Her voice was quite normal.

After an uncomfortable silence she spoke again. "You see, I'm not alone, Nick. Not alone in my sorrow. My friends are here. To comfort me."

Nick could think of nothing to say.

"Everybody has been marvelous," Letty went on. "The producers say I can go right into rehearsal. There's no problem anymore. Because the inquest ruled out foul play and now everything is fine."

"Of course she can go into rehearsal." Bacchus took up the subject briskly. "It would be absurd to cancel now."

"They couldn't get out of the contract if they wanted to," Dr. Jackman suddenly said. "Midge and I went over it last night, and unless they're pretty good—"

Letty took some of her drink and turned back to Nick. "You found him, didn't you?" she said. "You found him out there in the court."

"Oh, Letty!" Midge murmured with mournful reproach.

26

"Can't you stop watching me?" Letty demanded viciously, turning on her. She came back to Nick. "You found him when you got home that night."

"Letty, dear—" Midge again. "Please, dear, don't drink too much of that."

"I'm all right." She set the glass down. "Did you ever hear of the I Ching, Nick? It's an ancient book. Older than all our civilization, so they say. Everything is in it, Nick. Everything that ever happened, and everything that ever—"

"*Jesus!*"

Dr. Jackman rose on shaky legs, glaring. Midge gave him icy eyes across the room and he cried out in a wavering, cracked voice, "Then get her to control herself!"

"A little control all around wouldn't hurt," Bacchus observed.

Keith bent and retrieved the doctor's sandwich from the rug.

"Well, everything is fine now," Letty went on conversationally. "The producers say I can go right into rehearsal." She stopped. "I already told you that, didn't I?"

"You did, dear," Midge agreed fondly.

"Kenneth hated the play," Letty said. "He hated my being in it. He was a playwright himself, you know. Did you know Kenneth wrote a play? A play that was produced? On Broadway?"

"Yes, I believe I heard—" Nick hesitated politely. "A very good play, I understand."

Her lips began to tremble. She shook her head painfully. "No, it wasn't very good," she said. "It only ran four nights. Nobody came to see it." She stood up and said hoarsely, "Christ, does it matter? The man is dead. Doesn't anybody care? Doesn't anybody give a damn?" Weeping, she crossed the room, treading on newspapers, pushed open a door and disappeared.

With a distressed exclamation, Midge followed her.

"The poisonous little toad!" Keith Tilden burst out violently. "She ought to be glad he *got* it!"

It was a shocking outburst, and Bacchus said tonelessly, "That's a very stupid remark, Keith."

"Shit, I don't have to watch my words!" the boy exclaimed

arrogantly. "The police aren't listening to us now. Nobody knows why she put up with that rotten little—. Everyone hated him. Everyone!"

Bacchus said coldly, "I didn't hate him. So you're wrong there."

Keith started to reply, kicked savagely at the carpet instead and flung off to the other end of the room. He remained there, looking moodily through a window.

Bacchus sat down heavily. "We're all on edge," he sighed. "The damned newspapers won't let up. Here! Take any one of them!" He picked up a paper at random and handed it to Nick. "SUSPECT FOUL PLAY IN STRAMM DEATH PLUNGE" was the headline splashed across the front page. Featured was the now-familiar police photograph of the grisly scene in the court. There was also a full-length photo of Letty in the slinky gown of another decade. "*Tigress*?" Nick looked up inquiringly.

"Title of her first hit," Bacchus said. "I did the sets. She played a murderess in that one."

"She was always getting parts like that," Dr. Jackman said. For some reason the remark startled everyone.

"All this when the poor girl is trying to make a comeback." Bacchus lowered his voice because of Keith. "Every paper in town is raking up the old scandal. What can you expect?"

Instinctively they both glanced at the photograph on the piano. John Keith Tilden. The husband. The genius. He had quietly blown his brains out one summer evening five years ago. The event, unfortunately, had taken place before Letty's eyes. And there were relatives and friends of Tilden who still claimed that Letty had pulled the trigger.

"Now this!" Bacchus sighed. "And God knows where it will end."

"Can she really go into rehearsal?"

"I hope so," Bacchus said gloomily. "We've got no show without her."

Nick had just decided to leave when Midge opened the bedroom door and whispered that Letty wanted to speak to him.

She was lying on the bed at the other side of the room and it

28

took a moment or two in the semidarkness to make out the dark red of her robe. She held out her hand as he drew near, whispering, "I'm sorry I made a scene, Nick. I'm a little drunk, I think. And Ralph gave me something too. Something to make me sleep."

"That's what you should do," Nick said.

"But don't go yet," Letty begged. "Stay with me a little, Nick. Talk to me. Help me." She was crying, her head turned aside on the pillow, tears spilling from under her closed lids.

Nick sat beside her, holding her hand, and after a time she took it away and dabbed at her eyes with a damp handkerchief. "You're a nice boy to come and see me this way," she went on in a more normal voice. "How long has it been? Two years?"

"Almost three."

"You haven't changed at all." She managed a shaky laugh. "You're still quite devastating, Nick."

"You're kind."

"Is it true you and Petra have separated?"

"Yes, it's true."

"I'm sorry about that. She was so lovely."

"Yes. I'd rather not talk about it, though."

She lay back, watching him. The robe had slipped away from one of her shoulders. In the heavily curtained room her skin, her teeth and the whites of her eyes all had the same indefinite almond tone.

"Bacchus tells me he invited you that night," she finally said. "Why didn't you come?"

"What for?" Nick asked. "To wish you happiness?"

"Would that have been so hard?"

He did not answer. She raised herself a little, trying to read his face in the semidarkness. She could not make it out, and fell back with a hard laugh, saying, "Well, if you wished me the opposite, Nick, you got your wish!"

"I have always wished you well."

"Have you?" She smiled listlessly. "It doesn't matter anymore. That part of life is over for me now."

"Over? Did you love him that much?"

"Oh, love, love!" She stirred irritably. "Everybody talks about it as though it mattered." She stared ahead and said, "I never loved him at all. That's why it happened."

He thought she would tell him something more, but she reached for his hand, pressed it convulsively and whispered, "Don't go. Not yet. Don't leave me."

"I won't," he promised.

She calmed down, and in a little while asked him drowsily to open the window. When he turned back, her breath was coming light and regular. He quietly opened the door and left her there sleeping.

Midge was talking to someone on the telephone in the living room, Keith slumped down into a chair with a magazine. A uniformed maid walked around collecting coffee cups and emptying ashtrays. The doctor was nowhere in sight.

Bacchus had an appointment uptown and Nick left with him. Midge, still on the phone, blew them an abstracted kiss as they passed under the archway.

Outside on the street the reporters were gone.

"There's something I've been meaning to tell you," Nick said abruptly as they waited together on the curb. "It's about Keith. He lied that night. He lied to those detectives."

It brought Bacchus quite around. "Lied? About what?"

"He and that girl didn't go to the Dakotas that night."

"Why do you say that?"

"Because I would have seen them. I was there myself."

"I see." Bacchus thought about it. "In that case you also lied."

"Under the circumstances I could hardly do anything else," Nick reminded him. "Those men were gunning for Keith, looking for any chance to take him apart. I had to lie."

Bacchus pursed his lips, conceding it.

"I had to lie," Nick repeated thoughtfully. "But why did Keith lie?"

"There's one good way to find out," Bacchus said with a laugh. "Ask him."

"I thought maybe you would do that," Nick put forward mildly.

"Did you?" Bacchus was scanning the line of moving vehicles. "This is an ugly business, Nick. It may get worse. Why don't you stay out of it?"

"Stay out of it!" Nick's temper was beginning to rise. "With my name splashed across every newspaper in town? I'd like to *get* out of it!"

"Then do it, man! Get out of it!" Bacchus jerked a chin toward the great glass doors of the hotel. "*That's* not the way out of it!"

"You mean—Letty?" Nick was at a loss.

"Was it really necessary to see her? At this time?"

"It seemed only decent," Nick said. "I don't see how it gets me involved in any way."

"Oh, if you don't see *that*—!" Bacchus violently pushed air aside with a palm. It was the gesture with which one disposes of a fool past all saving.

The doorman had whistled up a taxi for Bacchus, but Nick held him back, saying confusedly, "I don't understand! What is it you're trying to tell me?"

"Don't come to me with your questions, Nick," Bacchus said. "You're not a suspect. We are. All of us. Remember that."

He got into the taxi and shut the door. A moment later the driver swerved into the traffic line and moved off.

Nick remained where he was, feeling rather stunned. His very good friend Bill Bacchus had just turned on him the face of an utterly ruthless stranger.

The Unexpected

Trouble is at hand.
Be careful all day long.

"It's nice. Really nice," Petra said. She looked in on the kitchen and dinette and turned back to the living room again. "It really looks comfortable, Nick." She walked about, touching things. "But isn't it awfully small? I would suffocate, I really would!"

"I had to find something fast," Nick said. "This seemed all right."

"Of course you had to move out of that studio. I'm amazed you can go there at all." She looked around again. "This is really fine, Nick. I'm just used to all that light and air in Woodstock."

She sat down and swallowed some of the coffee Nick had

made for her. She was a small-boned girl with a cap of fine blond hair and eyes of a very clear light brown. She had dressed for her visit to New York in the same tweed coat and skirt she wore in the country.

"You sounded upset when you called," Nick said. "What exactly happened out there?"

"Those two men came. That's all. They were very friendly, very pleasant—but they scared me."

"But what in the world did they want?"

"Well, the general idea seemed to be that you had walked out on me, and that I would therefore . . . cooperate." She smiled, her face going rather frozen and tight.

"In what, for God's sake!"

"I didn't know, myself. Then I realized they were pushing me, Nick. They were trying to make me say you disliked Kenneth Stramm, that you hated him."

"That's crazy," Nick said slowly. "Why should I have hated him?"

"Because of Lorette."

The name hung between them.

"They took it for granted I knew about Lorette," Petra said. "Since it seems everyone else did."

"Petra, it wasn't anything." He was wishing with all his heart she hadn't had to know this. "It wasn't important. To either of us!"

"I knew about everyone else," Petra said. "I just didn't know about Lorette. I—I *liked* her!"

"It didn't mean anything," he repeated helplessly. "It was over before it even began."

"Oh, I don't care about it," she assured him. "But I can't figure out when you got together. You must have both been so *clever!*" She searched his face and made a guess. "Was it when I went to Wisconsin? When my father was sick?" He could not make himself answer, and she turned away, upset. "When I went to Wisconsin!" she muttered. "I suppose I should have known!"

He tried to take her hand, but she snatched it away. "Oh, how

33

I loathe myself for caring," she cried wildly. "What is it I want to get back? Your insane selfishness? Your coldness?"

"I can't feel I treated you as badly as all that!" Nick protested.

"You tortured me!" she shrieked. "I had nothing! For ten years it was *your* work, *your* needs, *your* moods. I didn't live," she wailed. "Only *you* were allowed to live!"

Nick sat down and said, "Well, you're free of me now." A deathly weariness was coming over him.

"Yes, it's over," she drearily agreed. She took out a comb and ran it through her hair, staring into the mirror on the mantelpiece. "They're trying to frame you, Nick," she said dully. "You'd better do something about it."

"It's the craziest damn thing I ever heard! I was nowhere near the house until five o'clock that morning."

"Can't you prove it?"

"Why should I?" he returned angrily. But his thoughts were on Keith Tilden. He had not seen Keith since that day at Letty's hotel. When Nick came home that day Keith had moved out of Washington Street, leaving half his stuff behind him. He had not showed himself since.

He came out of his thoughts. Petra was gazing at him. Controlling impatience, he asked what was on her mind.

"I'm just curious." A pause. "Have you seen her?"

"Who do you mean?"

"Lorette. Have you seen her again since this happened?"

"No, I haven't seen her." He turned away.

She shrugged. "You must have been in love with her."

"I was never in love with her."

"You can marry her if you want to, Nick." The brown eyes filled. "I'll give you a divorce."

"I haven't asked for a divorce! For God's sake, Petra, get off it!"

The harsh assurance quieted her. She was calmer and more friendly after that, and when Nick took her to the door, she told him she was beginning to paint again. "I think you'd like what I'm doing, Nick. I'm really getting somewhere. I've broken through."

"I'll come out soon and have a look."

"That would be great." She gave him a sidelong glance, and added, "Be sure you bring along the next Mrs. Armisen."

"Aaah, now! Come on!" He gave her a little scolding hug. "There isn't going to be any Mrs. Armisen but you."

He had hit the right note at last. Her face cleared. She looked quite pretty again, and her smile was almost the old gay flash as she waved at him from down the hall.

He shut the door, sorry for her, yet relieved that she was gone. It was always bad when he saw Petra. But he was spared the usual spasms of pity and guilt. He was too disturbed by her news.

Two men, she said. It was probably the same two. Goodine and Shellman. They sounded like an old-time vaudeville team.

Where in the world, Nick wondered, had they unearthed that long-forgotten incident with Letty Tilden? And were they really trying to build a case against him on anything as flimsy as that? Turn and twist it as he would, the thing seemed too insane. He told himself that Petra had misunderstood, that there must have been some harmless and logical explanation for the visit of these men.

But the same day someone called Nick's name on the street. Turning, he saw George Maxfield coming through the traffic on University Place at a middle-aged trot. "Where the hell you keeping yourself, Nick?" he demanded, puffing. Maxfield was in his early fifties. He looked and dressed like a successful businessman. Nick thought him one of the best painters alive.

"I've moved," Nick told him. He wrote his new address on a scrap of paper and told Maxfield he must come over soon with his wife.

"Sure, Nick—but listen!" The painter lowered his voice. "Fact is, some son of a bitch was nosing around the place this morning."

Nick's eyes narrowed. "Police?"

Maxfield nodded vigorously. "Spotted him the second I opened the door. Dark guy, with a squarish face."

"What did he want?" It sounded to Nick like Shellman—the one he didn't like.

35

"He wanted just about everything. He knew about the shindig I gave over at the loft that night. Asked me what time you left, who left with you—"

Nick ran a hand through his hair. "What did you say?"

"Christ, Nick! I didn't know what to say! I told him I was too damn drunk to remember. More truth than poetry, eh?" He laughed, his eyes worried. "They trying to pin something on you, Nick? Hell, we were together all that night. I told him so."

"I'm not sure what they're trying to do," Nick said. "It might not mean much." He was badly worried and Maxfield saw it.

"Is there something I should have told him?"

"You did fine. The less said the better, I guess."

Maxfield looked at him, gnawing at his lower lip. "What about these people, Nick? You know them. Was there any funny business that night?"

Nick hesitated. "Nobody knows for sure. It looks bad because he fell out backward. But that doesn't have to prove anything. He might have felt himself falling and hung onto the window handles for a second or two, trying to get a better footing on the sill. That way his body would *turn*. He might end up falling out backward even though he originally pitched out forward. All that was established at the inquest."

"I guess that's fine then." Maxfield looked worried.

"They found Stramm's fingerprints on the window handles, so that part was all right." Nick paused and said, "Of course, he could have opened the window earlier. So the prints don't really prove anything."

"Nothing ruled out. Is that it?"

"Nothing ruled out."

"What about this actress? Isn't she a friend of yours?"

"Letty Tilden?" Nick was not sure how to answer.

"She's a good dame, right? And she's being crucified!" Maxfield clenched his fist at the injustice of it.

"Letty is all right," Nick said.

"Well, listen, I'll go all the way for you. You know that."

"Thanks, Max. Keep in touch."

He walked away, too sobered for fear. If the police were

making the rounds of all his friends they would find out soon enough that he had left Maxfield's party at two o'clock that morning and not at four. That left two hours unaccounted for. Somewhere within those two hours Stramm had died. It was becoming imperative that Nick find Keith Tilden and straighten out that business of the Two Dakotas. He walked on grimly, making his way westward to Washington Street.

Bacchus was sitting over lunch in his breakfast room and Nick told him without preamble that the police had been questioning both Maxfield and his wife. Bacchus looked very grave and said he was sorry to hear it. He was in no position, however, to offer any help. Keith was gone. He had left no address when he moved, and Bacchus had neither seen nor heard from him since. "You might ask Midge about it," Bacchus suggested. "Or better still, Letty. She would certainly know where Keith is keeping himself."

"I'll get no information from Letty or Midge," Nick answered coldly. Bacchus shrugged to show his helplessness. Nick turned away with bitter thoughts.

As soon as he was in his studio he put in a call to Harold Lasher. This attorney had a long-standing friendship with both Bacchus and Letty, and he had been particularly useful to Letty at the time of her husband's suicide. Nick had met Lasher socially on a number of occasions. He had also talked with him at length when the lawyer rushed down to Washington Street on the day of the tragedy. Lasher had kept close, if unofficial, tabs on the case ever since. He had offered Nick his services if he should ever need them—and Nick felt he needed them now.

Lasher came to the phone immediately. He listened to Nick with the total attention that had sent him to the top of his field, but after collecting the facts, he did not judge the matter as serious. "They're checking up on everybody, Nick" was his comment. "That's part of their routine."

"They're harassing my friends—they've upset my wife—" Nick spoke with anger. "Damn it, Harold, do they have a right to do that?"

"Maybe not!" Lasher said with a short laugh. "But there's no way you can stop them. Giving your wife that piece of gossip was on the nasty side—no doubt about it. But it doesn't have to mean much. Someone gave them an odd piece of information. Or misinformation." He added this tactfully. "They wouldn't be bothering with it if they had anything real to go on." If Lasher felt any curiosity himself about the "odd bit of information," he did not show it. "I wouldn't worry, Nick. These men are just fishing for anything they can get. They have nothing on you, and they know it." After a pause his tone sharpened. "Is anything really worrying you about this?"

After a hesitation, Nick answered negatively.

"Then forget it." More carefully, "Of course if they bother you again, I want to know it."

They talked a little longer and hung up. Nick had said nothing about Keith or the Two Dakotas.

He spent the next hour trying to work but found himself staring out the glass doors instead. The court was looking like a graveyard again. It was no good trying to work, and he gave up finally and went over to see a painter called Jack Sleeman.

He and Sleeman spent an hour talking about Paris and Giacometti and then had dinner together at a steak place on West Fourth Street. Later, at a bar, Nick ran into a red-haired girl called Ellen France, who had been a student of his at the New York Studio School. Nick had liked her work, and she was pretty too. But he had not seen her in a year, and in that time she seemed to have picked up some violent political opinions. He promised to call her and left her looking disappointed at the bar. He could think of nothing else to do and went home at a depressingly early hour.

The maid had been in his apartment that day. She had left a note beside the telephone. "*Mrs. Jackman said please call. Urgent.*"

Nick stood a long time, looking at this scrawled-out message. Then he went into the kitchen and poured himself a drink from a bottle of bourbon on a shelf. He took this neat, poured himself another and carried it with him into the living room. Here he sat

38

down heavily, still in his overcoat, and thought about things.

Just how long had it lasted—that old episode with Letty Tilden? A week? Ten days? During that time it was Midge who had handled everything: the people who wanted to borrow money, the people who had written plays, the cranks, the frauds, the daily mountains of mail. Those long hours in Letty's big cool bedroom—it was Midge who had made them possible. Letty wanted her hours with Nick undisturbed. Midge arranged that for her. An invaluable friend, Midge.

"Mrs. Jackman said please call. Urgent." A telephone number was scrawled under the message. Nick crumpled the paper in his hand. He did not want to speak to Midge Jackman. Certainly he did not want to speak to her tonight.

He got up restlessly, half inclined to go back to the bar and see if red-haired Ellen France was still there. He was considering this idea when his phone shrilled out. He let it ring four times, and then picked it up after all. "Nick! I can't believe I've finally got you!" The voice floated over the wire, light, brittle and nervous. "I've been trying for days and days! Are you alone? Am I disturbing you? Can you talk?"

"Yes, I'm alone. How are you, Midge?"

"How can any of us be? You've seen the papers!"

"I know. It's been bad."

"Isn't it incredible? And there's nothing you can *do* to these people!" She went on in a nervous rush of words. "I can't tell you what a nightmare it's been. We're in rehearsal now, you know. And as if everything weren't bad enough, they've got this completely unknown girl in the second lead. The whole company is up in arms. She upstages the actors, steps on Letty's lines—not a cheap trick of the trade she hasn't learned somewhere. And Letty won't fight. She never does."

"That's too bad," Nick said. "Letty is all right, I suppose?"

"Yes, she's all right."

An awkward silence.

"To tell the truth, Nick, I was wondering if you wouldn't drop by. Just to talk to her. It would do her so much good. Even a half

39

hour would be wonderful. The schedule is mad right now, but we're rehearsing at the Broadhurst. You know where that is, don't you? The Broadhurst?"

Nick broke in coldly. "I'm afraid I can't get over to the theater, Midge. My own schedule is pretty heavy these days."

"I know you have your work," she said humbly. And after a silence, "Well, I thought you might want to know how things were with her. Since you did come and see her that day." Her voice trailed off, disappointed.

"I do want to know. Always. And if I weren't so snowed under right now—"

He hung up with a brisk little click. So Midge Jackman wanted him to speak to Letty. Nick saw no particular reason why he should oblige her. The conversation had angered him.

The room still seemed to echo with her light theatrical chitchat. There was something oppressive, something vaguely threatening about her having called at all.

Nick had always rather liked Midge Jackman, thought her an attractive, intelligent woman performing a tough job with admirable efficiency. Now, he was wondering if he had liked her that much after all.

The note was still in his hand. Nick uncrumpled the paper and read it again. *"Mrs. Jackman said please call. Urgent."*

If Midge had called him, it was because Letty wished it. Whether Letty had said so or not, the call was made because she wished it. But why? Nick had no way of knowing what Letty wanted, no way of knowing what was going on in her soul.

He was not too sure, for that matter, what was happening in his own.

Clarity–Insight

The situation is grave.
It furthers one to seek the help of a sage—
a man of superior intellect
and high moral worth.

The six lines, alternately broken and unbroken, made up a little symbolic picture. Working from memory, Nick copied the lines on the back of an envelope and passed it across the table, saying, "Can you tell me, offhand, what this represents?"

"Certainly," Edwin Grey replied without hesitating. "It's the symbol of 'K'an'—an I Ching hexagram signifying danger. Translated in most versions of the book as 'the Abyss.'"

"The Abyss!" Nick repeated thoughtfully. "Would that mean a descent of some kind? A plunge?"

"It might mean any number of things," Grey said. "Generally

41

speaking, K'an is an unpropitious sign—although under certain circumstances the danger can be avoided."

Having taken this in, Nick settled back in his chair. "Tell me, Edwin," he said, "what exactly is this *Book of Changes?* Is it magic? Philosophy? A handbook on behavior?"

"A little of each. It's an oracle, a book of divination. A philosophic work too, of a kind. At least some people think so."

"Oh, the young people swear by it. I know that. But is there anything really in it?"

"It's not altogether easy to say. The book can't be explained by our Western notions of cause and effect. But there's a great deal in life that can't be explained by cause and effect." He leaned forward, poured a little rice wine into Nick's cup, leaned back again and said lightly, "Do you believe in extrasensory perception, Nick? Predestination? Magic or miracles of any kind?"

Nick smiled at the question. "I neither believe nor disbelieve. Frankly, I've never paid much attention to that sort of thing."

"You're a painter, of course," Grey remarked thoughtfully. "Sculptors and painters very often have a remarkably strong grip on reality. The involvement with physical surfaces, probably. But I'm a mathematician, Nick. My universe isn't as solid as yours. In fact, it has a way of fading out, getting hazy around the edges." He made circular motions with his hands, and his pleasantly cadaverous face broke up into a mask of laughter at once wicked and childlike.

Grey was a bachelor with a chair in mathematics at Princeton. He went up twice a week and was reputed to have written an interesting book on Gödel's theorems. The two men had met when Nick was invited to show some slides of his work at the university. He and Grey had talked after the lecture, and liked each other. Grey had just done a paper on diophantine equations. Nick had once read something about diophantine equations. Grey mentioned a small understated sculpture that Nick happened to regard as one of his best. In a word, they got along famously. Since they both lived in New York and within a few blocks, they had continued to meet after that.

Perhaps three times a month Nick would saunter over to

Grey's rooms on Charles Street and spend a few hours there. He always enjoyed it. Grey was an odd, interesting bird who dabbled in odd, interesting things. He had delved into Zen. He had a small rather fine collection of Chinese scroll paintings. He knew more than most people about the *Book of Changes* and had entertained a group of Nick's friends one night, drawing up some of the hexagrams and explaining their structure.

"So you actually believe in this book?" Nick asked him now.

"Let's say I find it calming, when I am troubled, to surrender my mind to the wisdom of Changes."

After making an effort to understand this, Nick let it go. "What about this symbol?" he pursued. "What can you tell me about it?"

"Not very much. It refers to danger, but one would have to know the query, the situation, that drew the response. Two men might receive a warning of danger. One may be imperiling the success of a business transaction. The other might be imperiling the welfare of his country. Everything depends on the question—the context."

Nick frowned. "I don't know anything about the question. I know only that this hexagram was the answer."

"The message, in that case, must remain meaningless to us."

Nick was following his own train of thought. "If these six lines foretold danger—particularly in the form of an *abyss*, a fall of some kind—it had meaning enough. In the light of what actually did occur afterward."

Grey said, "Don't tell me this has something to do with the playwright who—" He was visibly recollecting the newspaper story.

"A number of things dropped out of his pockets when he fell," Nick explained soberly. "I found a notebook in the grass. This hexagram was scribbled in it."

"Yes, you discovered the body, as I remember. An extremely bizarre— Some kind of party, wasn't it? And the glamorous woman was there. The actress. The one who killed her husband."

"He shot himself," Nick answered mechanically.

43

"The lady seems to specialize in violent death!" Grey dryly observed. Immediately he regretted this, since she was Nick's friend. "I suppose she isn't very real to me," he said apologetically. "People aren't, somehow, when you've seen them in the movies."

"It's all right," Nick said wearily. "Everyone talks about Letty that way. It's become a sort of joke to say she killed Tilden."

"It was your friend who gave the party, wasn't it? The one who owns the house? The set designer."

"Bacchus. Yes. Letty and Stramm were running up to Connecticut next day to be married. Bacchus asked a few friends over to celebrate. I was invited myself, as a matter of fact."

"Lucky for you you didn't go! Who did, by the way? Did you know any of them?"

"I knew them all. Some better than others. It was a small gathering. Eight altogether. Midge Jackman. Midge is Letty's agent. Also her best friend. She came with her husband. Funny little man. A doctor. Very much under her thumb. Who else? An actor called Leo Arnaboldi. A Yugoslav. I understand Letty got him out of a D.P. camp after the war. And Letty's son, of course. Keith Tilden. Keith is a sort of non-paying boarder in the house, by the way. He's been occupying Bacchus's guest room for the last few weeks. Keith's girl friend was there that night too. Pretty kid named Bettina Hodges. Related in some distant way to Stramm. Rich family somewhere up in Riverdale. Sleeps over occasionally with Keith. That's the lot. Except for Letty herself. And Stramm, poor bastard."

"Well, what about it, Nick? Would any of these people have pushed the man out the window?"

"Any one of them might have wanted to," Nick said with a smile. "Stramm was a damned annoying individual with a nasty way of poking his fingers into everyone's sore spots. Nobody ever understood why Letty put up with him. Nobody liked him." Nick added in a somewhat lower voice, "The son seems to have hated him."

"Do you think the son—?"

Nick said slowly, "I don't know Keith too well. He's a moody

44

kind of kid, but I can't see him doing anything that vicious."

"What about your friend? The one who owns the house?"

"Bacchus? Out of the question."

"Still, isn't he the one who went halfway up the stair? Perhaps he went all the way up and gave our man the fatal shove."

Nick shook his head. "Bacchus is out. Not in his character."

"Well, there's always the lady herself," Grey suggested.

Nick gave this some hard thought. "Letty had no reason to do it," he finally said. "If she wanted Stramm out of her life she didn't have to throw him out of a window. She just could have backed off—not married him. What possible motive could there have been? Money? She was the one with the money. Jealousy? The man stuck to her like glue. *He* was the jealous one. No. I can't see it."

Grey laughed. "Is anyone left?"

"There's Midge. She would push God and his saints out of heaven if it was good for Letty. The doctor's an odd fish too. Very much under her thumb."

"And all these people were consulting the I Ching that night? Really, Nick, this is getting absolutely fascinating!" Grey was deep in a study of Nick's symbol. "We could almost put the whole thing together," he murmured, "with this hexagram as a clue!"

"But if the message is meaningless without the query, without the exact situation—"

"Oh, we could make a try at it even so," said Grey, more and more engrossed. "This little cross, for instance." He pointed it out. "It shows us this third line was *moving—changing*. There's a special message attached to that line. Why don't we see about that, to begin with?" He was up already, and running a long, well-shaped finger along a shelf of books. Finding the volume, he took it down, feeling at the same time for his spectacles.

"Here we are," he murmured. "Hexagram twenty-nine— 'K'an—the Abyss.'" He skimmed through something, muttering, "Yes, yes—'abyss upon abyss'—we'll come back to that in a moment. Right now I want to get to our moving line in the third place." He turned a page, adjusted his spectacles and read aloud.

45

"'The danger can no longer be averted. He falls into a crevice, and nothing can save him.'"

Nick stared. "Did you just make that up?"

"Not at all." Grey held out the book. "See for yourself."

"A *crevice*? Is that what it says?"

"Meaning a chink, a crack of some kind. Curious idea."

"But don't you see, Edwin? That's what did actually happen! He fell into a cleft, a fissure in the stone!"

"So he did," Grey said calmly. "The book does sometimes come up with these amazingly literal answers. Shall we go on? We should really have the general message too." Turning back to the page, he read aloud: "'Abyss upon abyss! Grave danger! Passions rise mountain high. Nothing can save him, for the road leads nowhere.'"

Nick shrugged. "I can't make head or tail of that."

"I'm not so sure." Grey pursed his lips thoughtfully. "Let's examine it a little. First of all, we have 'Passions rise mountain high.' That seems to indicate a violent clash of some kind—perhaps a bad quarrel. We have it again that 'nothing can save him'—and as we know, nothing *did* save him! Then comes something interesting. 'For the road leads nowhere.' Now, a man who takes a road leading nowhere is clearly a man acting against his own interests—wouldn't you agree?"

"Certainly he will *get* nowhere."

"Exactly. He has lost his way. But he has lost it, remember, on a *road*. A certain *course* has been chosen by this man. A useless course. In this case, we happen to know, a fatal course. Now an intelligent oracle does not inform a man destined to fall out of a window that he has chosen a fatal *course*. If Stramm were to die by accident, the I Ching could have easily told him so. I can bring to mind at least two passages in the book that would do. For instance, 'In the end misfortune comes without warning.' What could be more perfect? I also call to mind a prediction that reads, 'You die, but through no fault of your own.' Not quite as good, but still suitable. Our man, however, gets no such warning of mishap. On the contrary, he is told he cannot escape disaster because he is on a senseless *road*!"

"He has taken a course dangerous to himself," Nick suggested, falling in with Grey's idea.

"I'd say matters have already reached the point of no return. 'Passions rise mountain high!' The situation is out of control. Destructive forces have been unleashed. Our man should abandon his useless, ill-chosen road. He should retreat—find a better one. Instead he goes forward—recklessly, foolishly forward—to his doom!"

"Damn it, Edwin, must you make out such a case for murder?"

Grey rubbed his chin sheepishly. "It's only an interpretation. Probably all wrong. Much more likely to have been an accident."

"Of course it was an accident!" Nick insisted. But a moment later he broke out again, more violently. "Why the devil did he go up to the top floor? It doesn't make sense for him to do that!"

"Suicide?" Grey hazarded.

Nick shook his head. "Not even Kenneth Stramm would climb two flights of stairs in order to throw himself out of a third-floor window! No—something's wrong with the whole damned thing." He looked at Grey, his forehead puckered in a frown. "There's something I ought to know about this. I just can't get hold of it. It always escapes me."

"Oh, you must get hold of it!" Grey insisted, intrigued. "I'm sure it's terribly important."

Nick was searching in his mind. "I came home very late that night," he told Grey. "I wanted to make sure, you see, that the party would be over, that there was no chance of—of running into anyone. So I stayed away, didn't get back until almost five in the morning. I stood outside the house for a while—just stood there looking up at the windows on the top floor. And there was something I knew at that moment, something I can't bring back to mind."

"Oh, but you must try!" Grey urged.

"It's no use. It rises to the surface and then sinks back again. I always feel if I could only get hold of it I would have the key to everything."

Grey reflected, and then said, "In that case, why not try the book?"

He looked quite composed as he made his suggestion, and after hesitating in surprise, Nick broke into a laugh. "Hell, why not?" he said. "I'll try anything!"

Grey fetched out three coins, laid them beside the open volume and said, "There you are. Ask away."

"Anything at all?"

"If it's worth asking."

Nick took a breath and said, "Here goes, then. *Did someone push Stramm out the window that night? And if so—who?*"

Grey threw the coins out six times, consulted a chart in the book, looked up. "Very promising! You have received 'Sun,' translated here as 'Clarity—Insight.'"

To his own surprise, Nick's heart missed a beat. He shook off the irrational fear. Whatever powers Grey claimed for this book, it could not scream out a name at him. And, in fact, the message, when it came, gave hardly any light at all:

"Only the superior man," the message read, "should seek to penetrate those dark deeds hidden from the day. A man himself beset with chaotic, uncontrolled passions must not probe into this domain, for he will work only greater harm."

"I didn't get an answer!" Nick commented.

"But you got a warning." Grey laughed. "Are you free of all chaotic passions, Nick?"

"Afraid not."

"Then you are warned to stop concerning yourself with this matter."

"Everyone tells me to stop concerning myself," Nick returned with some irritability. "I'd like nothing better. I happen to be in this thing whether I like it or not."

"How so?"

Nick said carefully, "I had some reason to dislike Kenneth Stramm. The police are aware of it. They've been questioning my friends."

"About what?" Grey was astonished. "You weren't even in the house at the time, as I understand it."

"I could have been there," Nick said. "There's an automatic elevator in the hall. I could have come home earlier than I said. I could have gone from my studio on the ground floor to the top of the house without anyone else knowing I was there!"

"But can't you prove you were elsewhere?"

"I can prove it," Nick said. "But I would rather *not* prove it, you see. There are—complications."

Grey was looking very serious. "Have you gotten legal advice about this?"

"I've talked to Harold Lasher. He doesn't think I have anything to worry about. And he ought to know."

"I hope you're protecting yourself, Nick."

"That's important."

"I would say, it's essential!" said Grey.

He put the book back on the shelf.

They went over to McSorley's for a drink.

Coming to Meet

Boldly and of her own accord,
the woman comes halfway
to meet the man.

Standing center stage under the harsh rehearsal lights, Arnaboldi was beating powerfully on a drum. A girl was walking a wide half circle around him in rhythm to the beat. The girl moved sinuously in a long-legged stride, occasionally tossing back a mane of blond hair. She had a snub-nosed, sensual face. Her paisley dress ended where her thighs began.

Abruptly the drum stopped. Arnaboldi's arms dropped to his sides. The girl halted too. "What's this?" she asked in a low, harsh, insolent voice. "More of your craziness? Beat your drum!"

"What's the use?" Arnaboldi returned hopelessly. "You can see for yourself there isn't a soul." He came down to the apron of the stage and sat dejectedly on the steps.

"All the same"—the girl looked about—"all the same the Slave said this was the place."

"Who is the Slave to give the orders?" Arnaboldi demanded. "He's not the Showmaster." After a brooding pause he continued. "He never leads us to the good towns. Traveling shows are coining money. It's wartime. People want to laugh." Another brooding pause. "What do we need him for anyway? Years back the Slave pulled when the animals got tired. But the wagon is motorized now."

The girl said, "Beat your drum! Someone is coming!"

Arnaboldi got up and looked offstage.

An old man, a limping man and a small boy came on, halting after a few steps.

"You there!" the girl called in her harsh, effective voice. "Where is everybody?"

The old man said, "There's nobody but us three."

"We can see that!" Arnaboldi said impatiently. "Where are the others?"

"There are no others. They've gone."

"All? Why?"

"Because of the enemy. The enemy is just outside the town."

Arnaboldi broke out angrily, "A fine thing! Where's your army?"

"They went off too. A long time back."

The girl came forward. "Hey! You with the limp! Where are they—the enemy?"

The limping man pointed. "Just around that bend in the road."

Arnaboldi, in a low voice full of dread: "As near as that?"

A voice from the auditorium called, *"Hold it!"*

The actors waited, relaxing. Arnaboldi dusted off his tights. He was wearing an acrobat's singlet with short sleeves. Joe Lechay, the director, came up on the stage and began restaging

51

something in the scene. He was a darkly good-looking man who looked thirty-five but was actually ten years older.

"The girl isn't bad," Nick said, looking her over.

"She's clever," Letty admitted. "She'll do well."

"She's not exactly pretty, but she's got something."

"They don't have to be pretty anymore," Letty said.

They were standing on the stage but out of the rehearsal area. Letty was waiting for her cue to go on.

"It's very simple," she said to Nick. "I want you to be my friend."

"No reason why I can't be that," Nick said.

"I need friends now. Very badly." She was looking out at the stage.

"I'm sure you do," Nick smoothly agreed. "But—are you really so alone?"

She frowned. "More so than you think."

"Look here!" Nick addressed her more directly. "Have the police been annoying you?"

She waited a moment. "They've been bothering Ralph Jackman."

"Harold Lasher says they're just trying for anything they can get. He thinks they'd have dropped it weeks ago if not for the newspapers."

"Oh, the papers are out to ruin me," Letty agreed carelessly. "They didn't succeed five years ago, and they mean to finish the job this time."

"Well, I'm your friend," Nick largely declared. "I'm at your disposal. What is it I can do for you?"

"I don't ask very much. Just to see you now and then. Just not to feel—utterly distant."

"That's very touching, Letty," Nick said.

She flushed. "You don't trust me. I know that."

He laughed. "My dear girl, the whole thing is clear as day! You've been told I lied for Keith. You want to make sure I go on lying for Keith."

"I do want that," she said calmly.

"Then why all this talk about friendship?"

"It's not talk. Is it so hard to believe I wanted to see you?"

"Yes—about Keith."

"That wasn't my only reason."

He laughed again. "You have too many reasons, Letty."

"I admit I've more than one." She spoke again, her eyes on the stage. "I was very much in love with you, Nick. But if you remember, you offered absolutely nothing."

"Only my very honest uncertainty."

She deliberated. "That wasn't much."

"You preferred the man you were sure of. You can't be blamed for that."

"It was weak of me. But Kenneth loved me. I needed his devotion." Her eyes filled. "I could count on his devotion!"

But Nick had not come here to be caught up in Letty's beautiful emotional storms. "And now you need mine," he rather brutally reminded her.

The actors were regrouping and she seemed not to hear him. "Will you wait?" she asked hurriedly. "This will soon be over. I do want to talk to you."

He said, with some hesitancy, "I want to help you, Letty, but I'm not sure I can. I'm in difficulties myself, as it happens. And too much is being kept from me."

"I'll tell you everything!" she promised.

"I'll have to know much more," Nick insisted.

"Yes! Yes! Just stay!"

The stage manager called out, "Your cue, Miss Harris."

Letty stepped forward and in a clear vibrant voice delivered her opening offstage line: "Hey, Clown! Do you want us to starve altogether? Beat your drum!" Entering the rehearsal area, she crossed upstage, looked over the three townspeople, turned to Arnaboldi and said, "Is this the best you can do? There can't be a penny among them!"

Nick watched her as the scene continued. A transformation known only to the theater had taken place. Since the leading lady is expected to be young and beautiful, Letty had become so. Trimmed down to the slimmest of little black Paris suits, she looked marvelous—even better than she had when Nick had first known her. Only her manner was not the same. She seemed less certain of herself, and her eyes were shadowed, tragic. She was the only one in the cast who did not know her lines. The other actors did not seem to mind, perhaps it was the privilege of the star. But Nick worried each time she had to be prompted.

The play, in the new manner just coming into fashion, presented a puzzle in place of the old-fashioned moral. Following the cryptic dialogue, Nick gathered that a Slave, a sort of Caliban, had in some manner gotten control of a small traveling show. Hating the Showmaster and his mistress (Letty), the Slave was gradually bringing about their ruin. Set against the background of an endless and meaningless war, the reference to America's involvement in Vietnam was quite clear.

Nick watched from the wings as the scene progressed. The Showmaster, played by an actor called Clayton Collier, was persuading Letty that with the town evacuated, their only hope lay in giving their show for the enemy.

LETTY *(with dread)*: We never gave a show for them before.
SHOWMASTER: We're not the only ones to do it.
LETTY: They're horrible, everyone says. Like brutes.
SHOWMASTER: They're not pretty. *(Thoughtful)* All the same, we'll make money if we please them. They may even help us with the Slave.
LETTY *(frightened)*: Help us? How?
SHOWMASTER: We'll have to get rid of him sooner or later.
LETTY: Must it be *that* way?
SHOWMASTER: What other way is there? The girl too. She's in with him—she plots with him against us.
LETTY: Why does she do it? She hates him!
SHOWMASTER: She hates us more.
LETTY: But why?
SHOWMASTER: We gave her to him.

Nick winced at the lines. It was murder they were plotting on that stage. The Slave who was gaining control . . . Stramm too, had been a slave . . . A slave gaining power, gaining control . . .

"That you, Armisen? Thought it was!" Clayton Collier had just come off out of the rehearsal area. Collier was in his late forties, a ruddy man with big, regular, handsome features and hard-boiled actor's eyes.

Nick said the play looked interesting.

"What's the good of it?" Collier returned. "We'll never open. Letty was out the whole first week. Backers don't think she's going to make it." He stared ahead with his big actor's face. "People are saying now that Jackman killed him."

"Jackman? Why should he?"

"I don't believe it myself, but the police have been to his office twice. Everyone says he's going to pieces. Blabbing all sorts of stuff. He's in bad trouble already, everyone knows it."

"What was it? Abortions?"

Collier shook his head. "Reducing pills. He's never been much of a doctor. Just took obesity cases, mostly. They found out he owned stocks in the company that made the pills. It was all in the papers. They say he may lose his license."

Nick was remembering the little man with his curiously aggressive air. A man in trouble. Now the police were badgering him.

"I can't see Jackman shoving anyone out of a window," Nick said.

"Oh, I don't know," Collier returned surprisingly. "These weak little men can be nasty when they're cornered. Midge and Jackman had plenty to lose if Letty married Stramm. Stramm and Midge hated each other. Once Stramm got into the driver's seat, the Jackmans would have been through. No doubt of it."

"Midge has other clients," Nick said slowly.

"Small potatoes! She and Jackman have lived high on the hog for years now. It wasn't only agent's fees. It was the summers out on the Island, the little jaunts over to Paris and London and Rome. Oh yes, they had plenty to lose—both of them."

The actors were beginning to break up, and Collier excused himself. A few steps took Nick into a cluster of people talking on the stage. Here he was hailed by Arnaboldi. The genial little actor had changed into his street clothes and was now wearing a topcoat and a fedora hat. He told Nick some of the cast were having dinner at a restaurant down the street. His face clouded a little at Nick's reaction to this. "Perhaps you wanted to see Letty alone?"

Nick denied it. It suddenly occurred to him that Arnaboldi might tell him a great deal.

"What do you think of Lilo?" Arnaboldi asked as the blond actress walked by.

"Very attractive. Seems capable, too."

"A born troublemaker." Arnaboldi sighed. "Lechay lets her get away with everything. It's a shame."

"Is it true the play may not open?" Nick asked.

"Who told you that? Clayton Collier?"

"He said the producers don't think Letty will make it."

"Collier is a liar. He's had a better offer. He wants to leave the show himself." A pause. "Did he say anything else?"

"He said Jackman was being questioned and is going to pieces. Are people really saying he knows something about what happened to Stramm?"

Arnaboldi laughed. "The actors talk! What else have they to do?" A queer, muddy look had come into his eyes. He seemed intensely relieved when Letty came up, putting an end to the conversation. Within half a minute Nick found himself surrounded by smiling actors, all interested and even flattered by his presence. Everyone wanted to meet him, and he found himself shaking hands and trying to catch unfamiliar names. The fine-looking giant was Samuel Lucas who played the slave. An older woman named Sarah Hall surprised him by actually knowing something about his work. A rotund young man with horn-rimmed glasses and a helpless intelligent face turned out to be the playwright, Ed Lamper. Through the pleasant buzz around him Nick gradually understood that all these people were joining Letty and himself at dinner.

As they all trouped through the backstage corridor, Nick held Letty back a moment. "You're making this into quite a social occasion," he said in a low voice. "I thought we were going to talk."

"Later."

A flash of anger went through him. "Does that mean not at all?"

"It's just some of the actors. Please, Nick, give me time. I'm tired! I'm hungry!"

Her lovely vulnerability took all his strength. She had thrown a little black coat over her shoulders. Her face looked very pale by contrast. It was true she was tired.

They came out on the gusty, dirty midtown street. The actors joked among themselves, an undertone of tension in the air. Nick felt out of place, resentful of the time spent away from his studio. What had he to do with these people and their problems? The afternoon had been wasted, and now the evening. Letty would give him only evasions. She was laughing now, talking with the actor who played the Slave, and an older woman named Sarah Hall. Nick suddenly stopped. "Why don't you go ahead with your friends?" he suggested harshly. "I'm not up to all this."

Alarm sprang into her eyes. "What do you mean? Aren't you coming with us?"

"We'll talk some other time."

"No!" Her hand tightened on his arm. "I'll go with you. Now!"

"But you're hungry. You just said so!"

"They'll give us something at my place. I'll tell you everything, Nick. I want to!"

She seemed quite desperately to mean it. Nick shrugged and, with her hand still clutching his arm, hailed a passing cab.

"Letty!" Arnaboldi called over his shoulder. "Aren't you coming?"

She called back, "Go on without me! I have to speak to Nick!"

The little actor stood watching as they drove away, his eyes frightened under the jaunty fedora hat.

"Everything Bacchus told the police was true," Letty cautiously began.

Nick waited without comment.

"But—there were omissions," she reluctantly conceded.

"Ah—the omissions!" He waited again, giving her time.

She clearly was calculating how much she could safely give him. They were in her suite at the hotel, and she was facing him warily across a coffee table. "I wish you'd stop all this, Nick!" she broke out irritably. "Bacchus says you've turned into some sort of mad detective ever since this thing happened. You've questioned him. You questioned poor Arnaboldi today and scared him half to death. Ralph Jackman is more afraid of you than of the police. I wonder if you know how nervous you've been making us!"

"I wouldn't be doing it if you'd play straight with me!" Nick retorted. "You're asking a good deal of me, too—all of you. Before I oblige you at my own risk I have a right to know what I'm getting into!"

She wavered, made up her mind and flung it at him. "All right! There was a scene that night! A quarrel, if you want to call it that."

"A quarrel about what?"

"Does it matter?" She took a cigarette from a box at her elbow. "It was simply a—general unpleasantness. I don't remember now what it was about."

Nick was bemused. *Passions rise mountain high.* Wasn't that the phrase in that queer book of Edwin Grey's? "Who was it Kenneth was quarreling with?" he asked.

"I told you, I don't remember. Kenneth was always impossible, as you know." She was upset thinking about it.

He watched her a little. "Did it have anything to do with the I Ching?"

But she took it calmly enough. Apparently, she knew all about the notebook he had found in the grass. Nick reminded himself that these people told one another everything.

"Yes, we were playing with the I Ching that night," Letty admitted indifferently. "Why is that so important?"

"I don't know that it is important. Bacchus and Keith were strange when I asked about it. And that little doctor went into a panic because you happened to mention it."

"I mentioned the I Ching?" She had no memory of it.

"The day I came here to see you. You were upset, not really yourself."

"I was drunk." She frowned, beginning to remember.

"Well, you started to say something about the I Ching, and the doctor got up on his feet and told you to control yourself."

"Did Ralph do that?" She laughed without great amusement. "He must have thought I was going to crack up then and there. Everybody thinks I'm going to crack up. Maybe I am." She brooded. "Yes, we were fooling around with the I Ching. Kenneth didn't like it. He insisted on asking some fool question. Well, he got this strange message from the book predicting doom. It didn't make sense to any of us at the time. It was only later—later—when we found out what had happened—" She clenched her hands. A spasm of agony went over her face. "You see, the book told us Kenneth was going to die. It even told us *how* he was going to die."

Nick said gently, "I know about all that, Letty. But it was just a coincidence, you know. There is no magic power in that book."

She shook her head. "You'll never convince me of that."

A pause.

"So there was a quarrel. Did Stramm go at Keith too?"

"He went at everyone," Letty said shortly.

Nick let a little time pass and began again. "When did Keith and Bettina leave the house?"

"I don't know. A little after two."

"And where did they go? To that restaurant? The Two Dakotas?"

"Since you were there yourself," she returned coldly, "you know they did not go there."

"Where *did* they go?"

"Oh, but you see, I don't know that!" Her tone held a touch of insolence now.

"I think you do know," Nick said.

Their eyes held. She crushed out her cigarette, leaned back

59

against the couch cushions and said, deliberately, "Very well. I do know!"

"You refuse to tell me?"

"I refuse to tell you."

The audacity of it took his breath away. Yet, in an odd way, it made him trust her more. If she was playing a game, at least she was playing it openly.

"I must assume in that case," Nick said, "that Keith did not leave the house at all. That it was he who followed Stramm up those stairs. That a physical struggle took place up there. That Keith, with or without intending it—"

"No, Nick! No!" Fear leapt into her eyes. "Nick, I swear to you that Keith did not push Kenneth out of that window! I swear it to you on my life! I swear it on *Keith's* life!"

In spite of himself, Nick was silenced. If ever there was truth in a human face, he saw it now. It was blazing at him out of her eyes.

"I suppose I must believe you," he finally said. "But you're still not playing fair, Letty. Where *is* Keith? Why has he disappeared? Why did he clear out bag and baggage as soon as he knew I was on to him? Why isn't he here now? Why does he leave you to answer for him?"

"He hasn't disappeared!" Letty pleaded. "He's just somewhere in the East Village with Bettina. He doesn't tell me where he is. He won't take any money from me—" Her voice broke and she began to cry. "Nick dear," she begged. "Don't do this to me! Think what hell it's been for all of us. Think how we'll all be living with it the rest of our lives. What is it to you, after all? You'll walk away, you'll forget it—"

"I wish you were right." He got up, feeling wrung out. "I'm afraid I won't forget it easily as that, Letty. You see—I killed him."

"My very dear Nick!" She stared, bewildered.

"I did—in a way. It was I who asked Bacchus to have that balcony removed. It was my fault about the sculpture too. Those Cleveland people had seen a photograph of it in an art

60

magazine. They liked it and they wanted it. I had it carted in from Woodstock so they could look it over. If I hadn't done that, Stramm would have lived. It's not that bad a fall from the top floor. He would have landed on soft earth. It had rained that day. He would have broken some of his bones maybe, but he would have lived!"

"Oh, my poor Nick!" Letty said gently. "Is that the extent of your very great guilt?"

And laughing sadly, she held out her arms.

Toward dawn Nick came out of a dream, abruptly and thoroughly awake. A piece had just slipped into place. The missing object in the top-floor studio. It was Keith's sculpture, of course! Keith's aluminum mobile. *Forms in a Moving Environment*, the kid had called it, or some such sounding name. A great whacking thing it was, put together rather cleverly with aluminum disks of various sizes. Not bad either, compared to what some of these crazy kids were doing.

Bacchus, to encourage the boy, had put this aluminum doodad on display in his upstairs studio, where it could be admired by the guests that night. Nick had seen it there only a few hours before the party. It had stood against the wall, right next to that fatal window. Yet less than twenty-four hours later when they were up there with the detectives, the damned thing was gone. There was nothing in the space beside the window— nothing but a strip of tapestry tacked up on the wall. Thinking back, the tapestry had struck Nick as wrong too, badly out of key with everything else in that room.

Now he asked himself why the aluminum mobile had been removed. Where was it now? A thing that size is not shoved away somewhere in a drawer.

He lay awake, gazing at a patch of blue light coming in through the heavily draped window. The electric clock beside the bed whirred softly. Letty lay turned away from him, her dark head buried in the pillow.

Nick gently shook her naked shoulder. She stirred, muttering

61

something in her sleep. "Letty! Wake up!" Nick whispered softly.

"What is it?" she asked clearly.

"Keith's sculpture," Nick said. "The aluminum sculpture. It was up there in the studio that night. Who took it away? What happened to it?"

"Don't know, dear," she murmured.

He shook the shoulder again, gentle, but insistent. "But it was there, Letty! You must have seen it there! A big aluminum mobile. Why was it taken away?"

She turned quite around at that. She was smiling happily. Eyes still closed in sleep, she offered him her lips.

He took them with his own.

Holding Together

If they remain united in their hearts,
all obstacles will be overcome.

"Yang and yin!" said Edwin Grey. "With these two words we encompass all duality. Light and darkness—storm and calm— leader and follower—male principle and female— Duality! Equal, but opposite forces, each with its own great task to perform."

"Equal, but opposite!" Letty saw it all quite well. "And the forces, of course, must balance."

"They must balance," Grey said with a nod. "However, they do not always do so. We are all aware of times when one of these forces usurps the function of the other, seeks to rise above the other, seeks to replace, even to destroy, the other. In fact, these clashes occur in a cyclic, almost a seasonal, movement."

Nick wanted to know what happened when the forces clashed.

"Bad times," Grey answered with a shrug. "Too much storm brings flooding. Too much calm brings drought. In the lives of men there is treachery, intrigue, violence. Followers destroy their leaders. Leaders oppress their followers. The strong grow harsh, the weak turn devious and vengeful. We have chaos, darkness, dissension, war—what you will. The whole wisdom of the I Ching is built on this concept of immense forces moving sometimes with and sometimes against each other."

"Of course. The forces. One sees that. But"— Letty leaned forward intently—"but the book, after all, foretells the future!"

"It does that—among other things," Grey assented rather absently. He was looking for it as he spoke, his eye running along the shelf. "But the power to foresee may not be as miraculous as we all suppose. The future," he threw out carelessly, "is merely an extension of the present—isn't that so?" He took the volume down as he spoke and stood now, weighing it in his hand. "It's the *now*, the present moment, that we really fail so often to understand. How *can* we understand it? There is so much we fear, so much we hate, so much we desperately need. Our passions blind us. If we would truly look at what we and others around us are doing here and now, we would see very easily what must come of it."

Nick gave a shout of laughter. "You make it sound very logical, Edwin. Do you believe all that yourself?"

"Well, to a point." Grey looked a bit sheepish.

"And after that?"

Grey said quietly, "After that point logic stops; I must admit I can't altogether explain what occurs here."

The table on which he now placed the book had already been furnished with several other objects. Among these, the pile of yarrow stalks was perhaps the most novel in appearance. Two wooden trays had been set side by side, and these humble but curious vegetables lay across one of them. Writing materials had also been prepared. Two shiny new Chinese joss sticks, rising above this little collection, gave it a scary yet rather childish effect.

"This is all most impressive, Edwin," Nick declared. "I see you are going to give us the full treatment."

"It takes a bit longer with yarrow stalks," Grey admitted apologetically. "Still—I thought a certain traditional element—"

"Yes! Yes!" Letty broke in anxiously. "You must do it exactly as you think best."

"Then let's begin." And with the informality that characterized all his movements, Grey lit the two joss sticks, releasing a scent of incense into the air. Then he seated himself at the table and declared he was ready for the question.

Now that the moment had actually come, Letty could not seem to find words. After a brief struggle she asked if she must speak her question aloud.

"You may ask it silently," Grey said.

Given this permission, Letty closed her eyes. Opening them wide again, she said with a dazzling smile, "It's been asked!"

"We will count the yarrow six times," Grey explained. "Odd totals give us a straight positive yang line. Even totals give us a broken negative yin line. In this way, step by step, we arrive at the meaning of our problem and discover how best to deal with it."

Grasping a handful of the yarrow stalks, he transferred them from the full to the empty tray. "The operative word is *chance!*" he explained. "This first random division of the stalks will decide everything that follows!"

Nick came around to watch as he began the counting of the yarrow. This seemed to involve transferring groups of stalks with extreme rapidity from one tray to the other, and at regular intervals, in accordance with some queer custom, inserting several stalks between each of his left-hand fingers. At these moments Grey most oddly resembled one of the warriors in his own scroll paintings.

When he had counted six times and drawn up his six lines, he opened the book and read from the hexagram "Pi," translated as "Holding Together."

The hexagram gave some promise of success, but hinted at obstacles and demanded great virtues and sacrifices. Letty could make nothing of it at all. However, since she had drawn a moving line she received an additional message. Grey accordingly read for her the following poem in eight lines:

Life leads the thoughtful man on a path of many windings.
Now the course is checked, now it runs straight again.
Here winged thoughts may pour freely forth in words.
There the heavy burden of knowledge must be shut away in
silence.
But when two people are one in their inmost hearts
They shatter even the strength of iron or of bronze.
And when two people understand each other in their inmost
hearts
Their words are strong and sweet, like the fragrance of
orchids.

"How beautiful!" Letty gravely exclaimed.

Grey, pleased, told her the lines were attributed to Confucius. Nick was silent. He could not help wondering what her question had been.

"Your moving line," Grey now told Letty, "does more than give us a special message. It also tells us that change is at work in your affairs. The time of *holding together* is moving toward something else, something new. This will be revealed by a second hexagram."

"Must you count the yarrow again?"

"That will not be necessary. I need only replace your moving yang line with an unmoving yin line. This gives us, of course, an entirely different hexagram."

He was drawing it as he spoke. But after consulting the chart he must have betrayed a shade of hesitation, for Letty suddenly turned pale, got to her feet and said she did not want to hear any more.

"Then we will go no further," Grey smoothly returned. He shut up the book with a little snap.

66

Letty had brought the reading to an abrupt close. She seemed a little dazed to have done it. "The first message was so good," she stammered. "And the new one, you see, might not be good at all."

"None of the hexagrams are good or bad," Grey told her somewhat regretfully. "Every prediction, you see, can be true only for a time. We all meet with both good luck and bad. Neither of them will last forever. Ultimately, that's all the I Ching can teach us."

Letty gazed at him, somber-eyed. "What's the good of luck," she asked, "if it doesn't last?"

"It can't be helped," Grey said. "This is more a book of wisdom than a book of magic. It can help us understand the way life works; it cannot change the way it works."

But Letty shook her head, dissatisfied. It was magic she wanted, not wisdom.

The little party broke up soon after this. Letty had come down to Charles Street after a long day, and she was tired. But she had taken a great fancy to Edwin Grey and as she was leaving, promised him tickets to her opening night. "Actually, we're opening out of town," she amended. "The play is in terrible shape, and we may never get to New York at all. So my promise of tickets may come to nothing."

"Oh, you're sure to have an enormous success!" Grey predicted. "How can you not?" He was quite swept off his feet by Letty's charms.

Out on the street Nick asked if Letty were really worried about the play. She shrugged carelessly. "The actors think some nut may heave a rock at the stage. Everyone says the play is jinxed. I don't say anything, since I'm the one who jinxed it."

They were walking together, their footsteps echoing on the pavement. It was past midnight now, and not many people were out on the pleasant treelined street. After a little Nick asked if the session with the I Ching had pleased her.

"I got a very good answer." After thinking about it, she added, "But I'd rather not say what I asked."

"You don't have to do that," Nick quickly replied.

"It's just something I'd rather not talk about."

"No reason why you should."

She glanced at him and said irresolutely, "Well, I can tell you, I suppose." After gazing straight ahead, she brought it out. "I asked whether I had any right to be in love—any right to be happy."

And having said it, she walked on.

Nick said nothing. He was extraordinarily moved.

"But I'm sorry I interrupted your friend," Letty went on after a while. "He was about to tell me my future. Now I'll never know."

"Oh, well, the future!" Nick waved it away lightly.

They found the Mercedes where Letty had parked it, and she offered to drop Nick at his apartment.

He said, "Let's go back to your place."

She nodded and started the motor. It was always like that. She always gave him a choice—an out.

He sat beside her now, letting her guide the car through the midnight traffic. He was remembering the queer abrupt way she had cut the reading short, thinking that it was probably some change in Grey's face that had frightened her—possibly, even, a flicker of worry in his own. Grey had shut the book quickly enough, but not before Nick had recognized the terrifying symbol at the head of the page. Even he had felt a chill at the sight of it. "Holding Together" with its promise of love and happiness had moved—changed. The sign of Letty's future was K'an. The Abyss.

Nick had been seeing Letty for over a month now, yet no clear pattern had as yet developed between them. The evening with Grey was unusual. As a rule, they met here and there, snatching time together as they could. Letty was taken up with press interviews, television appearances, costume fittings, rehearsals—there were always a dozen hectic calls on her time. Nick, on his side, was working long days at his studio and did not give up his habitual late hours with his painter friends. Often he found his way to Letty's apartment only in the small hours of the morning. She was never too tired to receive him, never asked him where he had been or with whom, never even asked, when he left her, whether he would ever come back. She seemed willing to keep their relations endlessly undefined. When she spoke of their affair, it was always with a jest, as though it were a thing of the moment, a thing that would not last. Sometimes Nick felt she did not really want it to last.

She could not have behaved in a manner more calculated to hold him. In such an atmosphere a man could easily go on for a very long time.

As the days and weeks passed, the shadow of Stramm's death receded. The police, as far as one could tell, had dropped the case. Letty herself never mentioned it. If she had secrets, Nick had stopped pressing her to disclose them. He had decided to give her time, sure that if he waited she would speak of her own accord.

And, in fact, just before she left for New Haven, where the play was to open, Letty did speak. Her subject, however, was not Stramm's death, but an event that took place several years before.

Nick had heard a number of conflicting accounts of Letty's marriage and the tragic suicide that ended it. The most popular theory was that Letty had either killed Tilden with her own hand or had driven him to suicide by her faithlessness. Her friends told a different story. According to Midge Jackman, Letty had been the perfect wife and mother, the victim of a monster whose one purpose in life was her destruction. Tilden, Midge said, should have been in an institution. He was mad as a hatter and it was a blessing to Letty and everyone else around him when he died.

Bacchus, on the other hand, asserted that Tilden was not mad at all, only eccentric. Tilden, Bacchus said, was a genius. He had revolutionized scenic art in the theater, and gone on after that to make giant contributions in the field of industrial design. Bacchus called him one of the great men of his day. The tragedy

69

had come about, Bacchus said, because his day had passed.

Now Nick heard a description of the man she had married from Letty herself. Sitting at her dressing table, valises packed for the New Haven trip, she sketched her husband in a few quick strokes. It was a devastating portrait of a genius, an alcoholic, a man suffering from bizarre obsessions and fits of insane rage.

Three years after marrying the greatest man of her world, Letty had realized her mistake. Tilden had been worshiped in his own family. He tolerated around him only those who would give him the same blind worship. His power, his money, his enormous personal magnetism all were used to exact from those around him a total subservience to his will.

"I took it as long as I could," Letty told Nick. "Then I cracked up—went to pieces. There was a period when I didn't—behave very well. I guess I wanted to prove I was still there. Still alive! And I didn't care too much who I proved it with." Her eyes in the mirror met his directly but with a plea in their depths. "It was such an awful life, Nick! He took me out of the theater. I had nothing—I *was* nothing!"

"Was the theater so important?"

She shrugged. "It was all I knew. I was never up there with the really great ones, but I wasn't bad either. I've done some nice things—things I'm not ashamed of. Yes, I missed the theater. It was better than running around with Tilden's rotten big-money crowd."

"So you had some affairs," Nick prompted.

"Very stupid ones. The only one that lasted at all was Kenneth. I never knew why Kenneth made such a fuss about it all. Nobody else did."

She opened a drawer and began pushing aside an array of little brushes and jars, searching for something. Nick watched her. Her features were marked, definite, as they sometimes are in women who resemble a handsome father rather than a beautiful mother. But there was exquisite delicacy in the high-bridged nose, the long line of the throat. And the dark eyes with their famous "frank" look held a promise unutterably feminine.

70

"What about Tilden?" Nick pursued. "Didn't he have affairs too?"

Letty said thoughtfully, "I don't believe John went in much for that kind of thing. He lost interest in me completely after Keith was born. What he wanted was mastery. He wanted me to bow down before him. He wanted me to think he was God."

"And you didn't think so."

"I knew he was an abject failure," Letty said simply. "He didn't forgive me for knowing that."

According to Letty, it was Stramm who precipitated the final tragedy. She had gone on with Stramm too long. He was beginning to hammer at her to leave Tilden and marry him. Letty had come to the end of her rope with both men. Receiving a picture offer, she accepted it and signed a five-year contract without consulting anyone. In the face of Tilden's wrath and Stramm's furious reproaches, she took her son and left for the West Coast. Hysterical letters followed from Stramm. Letty stopped answering. Stramm, then, did the one thing he should not have done. He lost his head, went to Tilden and revealed that he was Letty's lover.

This disastrous meeting took place at the worst possible moment. Tilden had quit the theater for the more lucrative field of industrial design. He had concluded a deal giving him part ownership in a giant manufacturing company. But Tilden's great innovation had already been digested by American industry; his ideas were no longer startling or new. The firm had decided to buy out his shares, scrap the plans he had submitted and use those of another man.

This killing blow to Tilden's pride was followed by the humiliation of Stramm's revelations. He went into one of his rages, and took the next plane out to the Coast.

"Was that when it happened?" Nick asked.

Letty nodded. "I had taken this place out at Malibu. I was giving a party that day, and there were all these people having cocktails on the lawn. John just walked in, and as soon as I saw him I knew something terrible was going to happen. I was deadly

71

afraid. The afternoon was coming to an end, people going off in their cars. Finally we were there in that big house—alone."

"And then?"

"It was a ghastly scene, of course. The worst. John was like a madman. He said he would not countenance my revolting liaison with Stramm, nor would he tolerate the 'degrading life' I was living in Hollywood. He ordered me to break my contract, come back to New York and take up what he called my duties as his wife. It was too much. I had to stand up or go under."

Nick waited while she took a long breath.

"Well, I told John I was not going back to him just to salvage his insane pride. I said I was through, that I wanted my freedom. I had talked divorce before, but this time he could see I meant it. He asked me if I intended to marry Stramm. I said I would do as I pleased. Well, he took out this revolver and told me I wouldn't have to worry about divorcing him. I thought he was going to kill me. I ran into the hall, screaming. That's when I heard the shot." She had lived with the memory of it for five years, and she spoke of it quietly and without emotion.

"Of course, I knew I was ruined," she went on in a matter-of-fact tone. "Tilden had relatives who claimed he had not shot himself at all, that I had killed him. It never came to a trial; Harold Lasher helped to prevent that. But I think now it might have been better if Harold had let things take their course. As it was, nothing ever really got settled, and I was simply dropped. The studio froze me out, stopped casting me, and finally I asked for a release. They were glad enough to give it to me. I packed up and came back to New York. Kenneth was one of the few friends I had in the world at that time. He stuck by me, he was loyal, and in a certain way that's when I began to care for him."

"It must have been about then that we met," Nick recalled thoughtfully. "You had that big apartment on the river. Bacchus brought me over one night."

"Yes, you came with your wife one night. And I fell. Hard. From the first moment."

"You got over it very soon," Nick reminded her.

72

She turned and faced him. "I can't believe you were really hurt!"

"Let's say I was unprepared."

"Nick, I'd been through so much," Letty pleaded. "Don't you understand? You were aloof, you never committed yourself. It was too hard to love you. I was too tired. I wanted to be with Kenneth, who loved me."

The sound of the buzzer in a distant room put an end to these revelations. A maid appeared in the door and announced that Mrs. Jackman and a gentleman were waiting in the living room, and that Mrs. Jackman had brought the car around.

"That will be Bacchus or Arnaboldi with her," Letty told Nick. "Both of them are driving out with us. Go and talk to them, will you, Nick?"

"How long will you be?"

"Five minutes."

A carpeted passageway with doors at both ends connected the bedroom and living room of the apartment. Nick stopped there for a moment, making sure in a glass along the wall that his long morning with Letty had left no telltale disarray on his person. Because of this momentary pause, and because the door was ajar at the far end, Nick overheard an odd bit of conversation.

". . . really wise to leave the city right now?" The voice had a trace of a foreign accent. Arnaboldi.

"I have no choice in the matter!" Midge, very sharp. "Letty is in no condition to go through this alone."

"But you're leaving Ralph in New York—leaving him absolutely on his own—"

With extreme impatience, "Ralph will hold up better than you think. You're all much too hysterical about Ralph!"

A pause. "What about this Armisen? Is he coming too?"

Nick, about to enter the living room, remained where he was, motionless.

"He'll be out on Saturday for the opening."

"She's crazy to let him do it!" Arnaboldi was getting excited. "This thing is just beginning to die down. His being there makes it a story! Doesn't she know that?"

"What do you want me to do about it?" With rising nervous irritability, "Damn it, Leo, I don't run her life!"

Although there was nothing in all this that could not be logically explained, Nick felt trapped because he had overheard it. He was particularly shocked by the hostile way Arnaboldi had called him *"this Armisen."* Nick had always thought the little actor liked him and was his friend. It was time to put a stop to a highly unpleasant situation. He did this by walking into the living room.

His appearance there created an extremely painful moment. Arnaboldi flushed crimson. As for Midge, her face "fell apart" in every direction; she looked almost comic in her surprise. Clearly neither of these two had dreamed Nick was in the apartment that morning.

They managed between them to keep a little small talk going, but it was all pretty bad. Things got a little better when Letty came out. They had the bustle of departure to help them, with Letty giving last-minute instructions to the housekeeper. Then the porters were carrying her bags through the living room and after that everyone was crowded together and going down in the elevator.

It appeared now that Bacchus had waited below all this time. He was seated in the back of Letty's gray Mercedes, looking more than ever like a Buddha. He and Nick exchanged greetings with a remarkable absence of pleasure on both sides.

The porters put Letty's bags into the trunk. Arnaboldi got in beside Bacchus. Midge slid behind the wheel. Nick and Letty waited on the curb. Since the others so visibly disliked his being there, Nick decided to compound their discomfort by kissing Letty on the open street, taking some trouble to do it rather well.

When he let her go they had lost awareness of anyone but each other. It was one of their moments. For that flash of time they were high above the world, demigods laughing on the golden slopes of Parnassus.

"I'll be out on Saturday," Nick said.

"Don't disappoint me," Letty said.

For a moment they smiled into each other's eyes. Then Letty got into the front seat beside Midge. Nick stepped back on the curb, his hand raised in farewell as the car pulled off. She waved back at him with a gloved hand, and as they rounded the corner Nick caught a last glimpse of her amused and beautiful smile.

Darkening of the Light

Entering the earth,
all light is extinguished.
Darkening of the Light
means wounding.

On Friday afternoon there was a sudden change in the weather. The sky took on a dark, discolored hue and a chilly little wind sprang up, driving in quick angry gusts across the city. In one hour the temperature dropped by fifteen degrees. Cold weather had finally come, with a promise of lashing rain.

At half past four Nick Armisen, alone in his studio on Washington Street, closed his skylight, turned on his lights and went on working. Nick was pondering some last touches in an almost finished piece and not sure touches of any kind should be applied. This hairline decision so preoccupied him that some moments passed before he was aware—through the rattling of the wind on his panes—of a repeated pressure on the doorbell at the front of the house. He went to answer it, wondering as he went who would be calling on him at just this time.

The man in the areaway was small and thin, with a thin, worried face and a bristly graying moustache. He wore a light tan overcoat, a natty tan hat and carried a briefcase.

"Excuse me, Mr. Armisen," he said. "I know I'm intruding, but I wonder if you could give me a few moments of your time." He was breathing unevenly as he spoke, and this gave his words an irregular and jerky rhythm.

Nick stared at him. "Why, isn't it the doctor?" he asked uncertainly.

"Dr. Jackman. Yes." He hesitated. "I won't detain you long. May I come in?"

"Of course!" Nick hastily threw open the door.

He had not seen Jackman for some time, and was rather shocked at the change in the man. He had always been thin and small, but now he was frail as a shadow, and his eyes, sunk deep into his skull, had a fierce, almost yellow glow in their depths.

He looked restlessly about Nick's studio without seeing anything, and could hardly be induced to part with his coat or his briefcase. He told Nick he had driven as far as Monticello and back that day and still had many things to do. He was clearly in a disturbed state, yet he exuded a sort of odd exhilaration. He had the air of a man who had finally come into his own, a man to whom, after years of gray nonexistence, something of import had finally happened.

"I don't want to keep you, Mr. Armisen," he began rather breathlessly. "But as it happens you are the only one who can throw any light on a strange—a remarkably strange—" He was feeling in an inside pocket as he spoke and, drawing an envelope out of it, he gave it to Nick, saying, "This came in the mail this morning. Will you look at it please?"

The envelope, already torn open, contained a single folded sheet of paper. This was blank except for six lines, broken and unbroken, crudely traced in a familiar vertical pattern. Nick examined it with a singularly unpleasant sensation.

"There is no signature," the doctor pointed out. "You'll notice, too, that there is no return address on the envelope. Nevertheless, Mr. Armisen, I am quite sure I know who sent it."

"But it's just some sort of joke, isn't it?" Nick was more disturbed than he liked to admit. "It can't be anything else!"

"No, it is not a joke, Mr. Armisen!" the doctor exclaimed excitedly. "It is not a joke. It is a threat! A threat on my life!"

"I can hardly believe it's anything bad as that," Nick protested slowly.

"Mr. Armisen!" The doctor was now breathing hard. "The night Kenneth Stramm was killed, his death was predicted by just such a symbol. You are aware of that fact. It was you—it was you—" He could go no further and finished by pointing with a trembling finger to the sculpture court outside the window.

Nick was conscious of a sudden violent desire to end this interview. "Yes, there was a notebook out there," he admitted coldly. "Something like this was scribbled in it." He added harshly, "I'm afraid I don't understand. What is it you want?"

Jackman pressed on doggedly. "You are familiar with the I Ching, Mr. Armisen. You are the one—the only one—who can tell me what I need to know. Is the symbol on that paper identical with the symbol that predicted Mr. Stramm's death?"

Nick thought about it. There was no doubt in his mind about the hexagram, which he recognized at a glance. It was, in fact, an ugly thing for Jackman to have received in the mail. It occurred to Nick, too, that he owed the man a straight answer. "I'm not as familiar with all this as you seem to imagine," he finally said. "But since you ask me, I would say, yes—it is the same!"

Uttering a hoarse cry, Jackman flung up both his arms. Strange to say, there was triumph as well as terror in that gesture. "Thank you!" he got out breathlessly. "Everything is clear now! I have been informed that I am to die—to die as Kenneth Stramm died. That is all I wanted to know. My letter, please!" He stuffed it into his pocket. "Yes, I know who sent it," he repeated with his strange embittered pleasure. "And I know why he sent it. But you need not worry about me, Mr. Armisen. I am not as helpless as some people may imagine. I have taken steps—steps to protect myself!"

"I'm sure it isn't as bad as you think," Nick said helplessly. There was, in fact, something naïve, almost childish, about the scrawl on the page. "After all," Nick went on, "is there any *reason* why anyone should—"

"Reasons?" The doctor laughed theatrically. He was gathering his belongings. "I'm not at liberty to talk about reasons, Mr. Armisen. I know what I know, and I'm not saying what I know. But I'll tell you this much: once the police get onto something, they never let go. They get at the truth, Mr. Armisen. Yes! The truth will out!"

Nick was silent. It had suddenly occurred to him that it was Jackman who had given the police the "odd bit of information" about himself and Letty.

Although he insisted he could find his way, Nick took him through the hall to the areaway door. It had grown darker while they were together, and a first fine slanting line of rain was visible around the streetlamps. The doctor had parked his car down the street, and Nick stood in the doorway and watched him make a run for it. He held on to his hat as he ran, his thin body listing in a wind that tore at his coattails. Nick watched him until he disappeared in the twilight. Then he slowly went back to his studio.

It was time to go home now, to prepare for the evening. He was dining with wealthy friends that night. Important collectors would be there, people of standing in the art world. Yet he stayed where he was, listening to the first staccato spatter of rain on the skylight.

He was suddenly aware that he was alone in this house on Washington Street. Bacchus had gone on with the actors. Neither his guests nor his servants were to be found on the floors above.

K'an. There was something uncanny about the way the

79

symbol kept cropping up in this affair. Had someone really sent it to the doctor as a threat? Had he in some way failed that queer little man? That strange yellow glow in Jackman's eyes. It was fear that had glowed there with so fierce a light. And behind the fear? Loneliness? A dumb plea for help?

Nick put his studio in order, went home to dress, and then made his way uptown to the home of his friends. All through the pleasant evening, the excellent dinner, the interesting talk, the thought of his odd visitor stayed with him, persistent as the rain outside. It was coming down now in torrents, coming down as though it would never stop.

The first thing Nick heard as he opened his eyes next morning was the rain drumming on his windows. A dripping leaden sky hung over the wet rooftops. It was the day of Letty's opening.

He lay motionless for a moment, then, with a single abrupt movement, swung his legs out of bed. He knew now exactly what he had to do, knew it without question. He threw on his clothes, drank down two cups of instant coffee standing up in his kitchenette and then went out into the rainy, windy morning. A quarter of an hour later he was entering the house on Washington Street. Without looking in on his studio, he rode the automatic elevator up to the top.

Keith's old workroom gave him nothing at all. Two closets in the hall, an unused bath and a makeshift kitchen at the back yielded as little. What he wanted was not there, and he ran down the stairs to the floor below.

At the end of an hour he had worked his way to the ground floor, systematically ransacking every closet, every cupboard, every foot of open or concealed storage space as he descended. He had come almost to the end of his search and wondered if he could be wrong. He cursed but did not give up. A service door here opened on a steep stairway leading to the basement. Nick went down the steps.

He found what he was looking for among the discarded, broken tools and miscellaneous rubbish in a low-ceilinged space near the boiler room. It had been hidden from sight under a heap of burlap sacks, and Nick's heart leaped with excitement when he uncovered it. Keith's masterpiece. The aluminum mobile. Badly off balance now, and with most of the metal disks lost or broken. But the central disk still hung loosely in place, and Nick noticed a small hole near the top of it. The area around the perforation was dented inward in a rather curious fashion. A lion now on the scent of blood, he flung the unwieldy thing aside and rode the elevator once again to the top.

The death window had been boarded up, but the strip of tapestry still hung on the wall beside it. Nick crossed the room in six steps and tore it down with a single violent movement. There was nothing behind the tapestry but a small hole in the white plaster wall.

A search of Keith's old worktable provided him with a chisel and a hammer. Returning with these tools, he began grimly chipping and digging at the plaster wall. The job took him fourteen minutes, and at the end of it a small shapeless bit of lead lay in the palm of his hand.

Someone had fired a gun in this room.

The call to New Haven went through smoothly, but Bacchus had already left the hotel.

After an infuriating conversation with someone at the box office, Nick was given the number of the backstage phone. This was answered by the stage manager, Jim Benson, and after an interminable wait by Bacchus.

"What bullet hole?" Bacchus asked, very collected. "I don't know what you're getting at, Nick. There's a rehearsal going on, and I don't really have time for this."

"I'm afraid you'll have to make time." Nick's voice was hard as nails. "A gun was fired up here. The bullet went through an aluminum disk of Keith's mobile and lodged in the wall. I've got the bullet. It's here in my hand."

In the silence that followed Nick could hear voices faintly reciting lines on the stage. Then Bacchus said, "I know nothing about it." His voice rose. "Nothing! Do you understand?"

"Come off it, Bill," Nick came back roughly. "The mobile

was carried down to the basement, a tapestry was tacked up on the wall, and you know nothing about it?"

Bacchus cleared his throat. "I know nothing about it."

This was too outrageous for comment, and Nick changed his tack. "Are you denying you own a gun?"

"Why should I deny it? I have kept a gun in the drawer of my bedside table for ten years now. It has never been fired. I don't know what you found down there in my boiler room, Nick—or by what right you have just ransacked my house"—his tone was loaded with anger now. "Since you suspect me of something criminal, I suggest you take it up with the proper authorities. I have no more time for this."

"It's Ralph Jackman who will go to the proper authorities," Nick cut in bitterly, "if he hasn't already been there!"

Bacchus was finally startled. "What? What? Jackman? When did you see Jackman?"

"He was here yesterday. He got an anonymous letter in the mail. He thinks someone is trying to kill him. I'm not so sure he's wrong."

"And it will be your fault if they do," Bacchus suddenly shrieked, losing his head. "You have meddled! You have meddled! And I will not be responsible!"

"I've had enough of this," Nick flung out, losing his temper. "Put Letty on the phone. She'll talk sense if you won't!"

"I'll not put her on," Bacchus retorted. "I'll not have her unnerved by your hysteria."

"To hell with this!" Nick said roughly. "You're a fool, and I have nothing to say to you. Put Letty on!"

"I'm damned if I will! You may not think it matters, but we're giving a show here tonight. And you're not going to destroy it!"

He disconnected with a violent clap.

Nick put the receiver back more slowly. He and Bacchus had been on cool terms for some time now, but they had never before confronted each other openly as enemies. He shook his head to clear it. A hard anger was coming up inside him. He had given Bacchus his chance in this thing. Bacchus had side-stepped. So much the better. Nick would deal with it alone.

After some thought he ran down the stair to the landing below, walked along a carpeted passage, and pushed open a door.

The master bedroom lay in its usual immaculate order. Plastic dust covers protected the gold chaise longue and the deep velvet armchair. Plum velvet drapes screened out the sunlight, and a pristine linen sheet had been carefully pinned over the vast violet satin counterpane. A New England lamp of green glass, a transistor radio of German make, a gold-bound appointment book and a tricky newfangled telephone were arranged, each in its proper place, on a cherrywood bedside table. Nick pulled out the one deeply curved drawer by its brass handle. The drawer opened smoothly, revealing inside the blue glint of Bacchus's revolver. A handsome and formidable little engine of death it looked to be. At the last minute Nick decided not to touch it. He was shutting the drawer when the telephone signaled shrilly not an inch from his hand. His nerves jumped. He picked up the receiver.

"Nick, what on earth *is* all this about Ralph?" Midge. Calling from New Haven. It hadn't taken her long.

"He received some kind of anonymous letter," Nick told her tonelessly. "He seems to believe it's a threat of some kind."

"Oh, for heaven's *sake!*" She sighed fretfully. "Can't you get him to calm down, Nick? What do you mean, an anonymous letter? What did the letter *say?*"

"It didn't say anything. There was nothing in it but an I Ching hexagram."

"An I Ching—you mean that crazy—? Oh, this is simply too much!" Midge sounded out of all patience. "The whole thing is just some ridiculous nonsense, Nick. It's nothing at all."

"Well, he seems to have been pretty upset by it," Nick said dryly. "He says someone is out to get him, and that he is taking steps to protect himself."

"Taking steps to—?" Midge was suddenly alert. "Protect himself how? Exactly what did he say?"

"Just that. I think he means to take the matter up with the police. He may already have gone there."

"N-no," Midge answered slowly. "No, he hasn't done that."

She was silent a bit. "I'll call him right away. I'm sorry you've had to deal with this, Nick."

"I haven't dealt with anything," Nick told her pointedly. "I thought you people might want to deal with it."

"You're quite right. I'll call him." After a pause. "Are you coming out tonight?"

"What? Oh! Well—I'm not sure."

"It's the opening. She'll be terribly disappointed if you don't."

"Where is she? Can I speak to her?"

"She's on the stage. We're having a technical rehearsal."

"How soon will she be free?"

"We'll break in about an hour."

"Tell her I'll call her at the hotel."

They both hung up. Clearly, Bacchus had said nothing to Midge about the bullet hole.

Nick was wondering if it was not a mistake to have called New Haven at all. These people were of no real use. All they cared about was their opening. "Keith!" Nick muttered aloud. "That's the boy I want."

He got into his raincoat and left the house by the big front door. The wind was blowing up hard now. Thunder rumbled somewhere on the horizon. The rain came down unceasingly.

The
Marriageable
Maiden

The young girl follows the man of her choice.
But undertakings bring misfortune,
for the lines are not
in their proper places.

At one o'clock of a rainy Saturday afternoon the Two Dakotas was already filled almost to capacity. A sprinkling of freaks and loonies gave the place an authentic touch, but it was mostly a well-heeled younger crowd that came—glittery young people making it in films, in fashion or in the new art. Fashionably disaffected, dressed in the mad styles of the wealthy avant-garde, they packed the place, black and white together taking up the tables and crowded three deep at the bar.

So many young bodies at such close quarters created a strong undertow of sex. Walking in, one felt the drag of it like a heavy swell at sea. Over the deafening uproar of voices the exultant sorrow of Aretha Franklin pounded the smoke-filled air.

Nick and his friends came in occasionally because the place stayed open late, because the food wasn't bad and because they gave you unwatered drinks. Nick had never been there so early in the day, but the Dakotas seemed to him as good a place as any to start. He had chosen it with a faint hope of running into Keith, but saw no one he knew at all and ordered a beer standing up at the bar. After a few minutes Louis, the owner, came over for a friendly chat.

They talked a little about people they knew, and then Nick asked if Keith Tilden ever came in these days. He had made a mistake and immediately knew it. A wary look sprang into the owner's eye. "I'll tell you the truth," Louis expounded with an air of candor. "I wouldn't know the kid if I saw him. When you get them in like this"—his gesture took in the crowded tables— "they begin to fade into the scenery." He went on pleasantly, "I do a lot of business here—fifty, sixty people standing up at the bar on a weekend night. The Tilden boy might have been in. I don't keep track." And with a nod a shade less friendly, Louis went back into the smoke and noise of his restaurant. The police undoubtedly had questioned him about Keith already. He did not welcome further inquiry.

Outside the Dakotas, the rain had stopped. Nick crossed the street at a run and caught a bus headed downtown. He rode it as far as Astor Place, and then got off and walked east.

The moneyed little world of the Two Dakotas lay behind him now. He was entering the streets of the Aquarian Age. A strange little revolutionary outpost it was, where among the run-down warehouses, tenements and broken paving stones of the past, signs and portents everywhere proclaimed the dawning of a new time.

He walked on past unisex barber shops, head shops, light shows, dark little health food restaurants. Dingy storefronts had been turned into theaters. Newspapers blazoning new truth operated out of basements. Posters were up everywhere demanding the release of unknown jailed martyrs. And just down the street a huge psychedelic rose reared up along the brick side of a tenement wall.

At the corner, a young man with the smile of a della Francesca angel offered Nick a nonverbal newspaper. This, as it transpired, was a four-page sheet, innocent of newsprint and covered on all four sides with pornographic drawings and photographs. The insane imaginings on the page, Nick understood, were not meant to stir his lower passions. On the contrary, they were a stern reminder that salvation lay only in Truth. Nick returned the paper but gave the young man a dollar with which to continue his endeavors.

All around him now were the shock troops of the future, volunteers in the last doomed battle for a better world, and all with the mark of Hiroshima in their young interplanetary eyes. There were mystics with matted hair and monks in hempen robes. There were blacks in dark ceremonial gowns. There were at least a dozen blond and bearded versions of the Savior Himself.

The girls beside them wore kindergarten muslins or the robes of Hindu priestesses. Their hair flowed in silken beauty down their shoulders, and they walked calmly in the dignity and perfection of their youth. All along the street exquisite young men courteously asked Nick for any small sum he might have about him, while maidens held out to him trays laden with painted ashtrays, beads, pots of incense and cunningly woven jewels fashioned of rope.

For over an hour Nick wandered these rickety streets with their signposts pointing to a strange new future. Twice he looked in on places that seemed to be exhibiting art. He saw a great deal to astonish him but no work by Keith Tilden.

At four o'clock he sought refuge and sustenance in Ratner's on Second Avenue. His mission was beginning to lose reality in his mind. He was asking himself what a crazy message in the mail, or even a bullet hole in a wall, had to do with him or with his life. He was about to give up and go home when a girl with long red hair called his name from one of the tables. It was Ellen France, and Nick went over to greet her. She was sitting with a group of friends, all of them respectfully silent as she pronounced his name. For Nick was looked upon as a great man by this new generation. Although they held only a small place in his world, he loomed as a hero of theirs.

The accidental meeting with Ellen France was Nick's first piece of luck. She knew Keith well, as it happened, and had dropped by at his place only the night before. In no time at all Nick had gotten from her the address he had sought all these hours.

Ten minutes after leaving Ratner's restaurant, he was pressing the bell of a walk-up on St. Mark's Place. The buzzer admitted him into a dark hallway giving off that depressing airless odor typical of all poor city dwellings. As he mounted the stair, Bettina came out on the landing and looked over the banister, a blond rope of hair over one shoulder.

"It's me, Bettina—Nick Armisen!" he called as he came up the steps. "I'm looking for Keith. Is he here?"

A polite little gasp from the landing. "Oh, Nick! He isn't home. I'm so sorry." She retreated a little as he reached the landing and told him again in her soft little debutante's whisper that Keith was out. She was wearing a faded blue flannel wrapper, and although it was late afternoon, appeared to have just gotten out of bed. "Do you know when Keith will be back?" Nick asked her.

"Oh, this is really terrible, Nick. He didn't say." After a moment she asked if he would like to come in.

He felt a sharp disappointment not finding Keith but, after hesitating, said, "Just for a moment, maybe."

He followed the girl into a kitchen, which apparently also served as living room, for it boasted a bookcase and a moth-eaten couch along one wall and the huge black-and-white face of Che Guevara staring out from another. A pile of unwashed dishes lay in the sink. She offered Nick some coffee from a pot on the stove, but he said he could not stay.

"Dr. Jackman came to see me yesterday afternoon," Nick abruptly remarked. "He got something in the mail that frightened him. An I Ching hexagram. Do you know anything about that?" He was too tired for tact and simply blurted it out.

"A hexagram?" She shook her head wonderingly. "That's funny! No—I don't know anything about a hexagram." She turned away a little too late—he had seen the tiny leap of terror in her eyes. But she was so soft, so without vital strength he hardly knew how to deal with her. Still, he had to try. "Bettina, look at me, won't you?" He spoke very gently.

"Gee, Nick!" She backed away from him. "What is all this? You're beginning to scare me!"

"I don't want to do that. But someone did send this message through the mail, and Dr. Jackman seems to believe he is being threatened. I've been disturbed about that, and about other things too. I may be in difficulties myself at this point, and I must have certain facts."

"What facts?" she quavered out. "What—what do you want me to say?"

"Do you mind talking about the party? The one Bacchus gave that night?"

"No. Why should I mind?" She had gone dreadfully pale.

"To begin with, why did you and Keith leave the house that night?"

She answered breathlessly, "Gosh, Nick, after all, Letty is Keith's *mother!* We'd been there hours and hours. We wanted to have some fun! Is that so terrible?"

"No, it's not terrible. But where did you and Keith go?"

She gave her little society girl's laugh. Was there a slightly brazen note in it now? "If we're going into all that, I'd like to have a cup of coffee." Turning to the stove she poured two cups, one for herself and one for Nick. She set them on the table, coming rather close to him as she moved about. Her robe had slipped, revealing an inch of lovely ivory-toned flesh. "Coffee?" she insisted lightly. "No? Won't you at least take off that dreadful wet raincoat?"

Something very still in his demeanor made her hands drop before they actually touched him. But she looked up, brazenly

89

laughing, into his eyes. "I'll tell you all about it, Nick," she said with a coaxing pout, "but you'll have to promise me—"

Nick felt rage mounting from somewhere inside him into the base of his skull. "I'll promise you nothing!" he flung at her harshly.

She was stung into defiance. "Then I'll tell you nothing!" she cried.

"Cover yourself up!" He rapped it out at her like a drill sergeant. "You're not dealing with some long-haired jerk you picked up down there on the street. You're going to tell me what I want to know, and you're going to talk straight for a change!" And taking her by the arm, he slammed her back against the wall.

She uttered a tiny scream and then stood motionless, panting. His own violence shocked him, and he saw with relief that she was not hurt, only badly frightened.

She was trying to say something, but her mouth quivered and she could not control it. Tears gushed out of her eyes. She sat down, put her head on the kitchen table and cried like a child.

Nick sat beside her. "Listen to me, Bettina!" he said desperately. "You may not understand this, but I'm trying to help you. I'm trying to help Keith. But I can't do it unless you tell me what I need to know."

"But there's nothing I can tell you!" Her voice rose hysterically. She tried to get up, but he grasped her wrist and forced her down again. She stared at him with frightened starlike eyes through a tangle of golden hair. She was trembling from head to foot.

"There was a quarrel that night," Nick said. "A bad quarrel. What was it about?"

She moistened her dry lips. "There wasn't any quarrel. Kenneth was in a foul mood, and—and, well, he got into this argument with Dr. Jackman—"

"Never mind about that. I want to know about the real quarrel. The one with Keith! Come on! Talk! They fought, didn't they? Didn't they?"

He was still holding her there by her wrist, and she burst into tears. "It was Kenneth's fault if they did!" she broke out passionately. "Keith was trying to be nice that night. It was just no use! Kenneth wouldn't let up, wouldn't stop needling him! Ever since Keith was a kid Kenneth has been doing that! Oh, yes!" she cried wildly. "Keith told me! Nothing he ever did was right, nothing was ever good enough. Kenneth was always playing the heavy father around the house. And all the time Keith despised him, and knew how weak he was." She dabbed at her eyes. "Well, Keith finally couldn't take any more of it. Kenneth was saying every rotten thing he could think of. He said Keith took drugs. And that was a lie. He doesn't. Not hard drugs ever! And then—then he said Keith was marrying a girl"—her tears fell faster—"a girl who wasn't right in her head. And I didn't *like* it when Kenneth said that," she exclaimed childishly. "I got upset, and I got up and ran out of the house."

"And what did Keith do?"

"He ran right after me! And he said, 'Tina! Tina, honey, what do you care? He's just a bastard!' And then"—the tears flowed afresh—"and then I told Keith I couldn't marry him. Because you see, what Kenneth had said—it was *true*." She gazed at Nick with pitiful mascara-smeared eyes. "When I was fifteen my parents had to put me into a—a mental place. I was there two years. I was going to tell Keith. I wouldn't have lied about it. But now everything was hopeless because Kenneth had told him instead. So I told Keith I couldn't go on with him because I was a mental case and a misfit and I'd never be anything else."

Nick took this in without words.

"But Keith didn't care one bit that I'd once been sick," Bettina went on, tossing her head proudly. "He just hated Kenneth more for upsetting me. He got white in the face, and he said, 'The murdering son of a bitch!'"

"*Murdering?*"

"That's what he said." She repeated it with satisfaction. "And then—" She stopped short, fearful that she had already given away too much.

"Keith went back into the house, of course," Nick muttered thoughtfully. "I always knew he must have done that."

91

"But nothing happened in there," Bettina said quickly. "Nothing. Keith came out a few minutes later and told me everything was all right and I should go home and not worry about anything."

"He came out? Hadn't you followed him inside?"

"No, no! I—" She faltered. "I waited where I was. On the stoop."

"Did Keith say Stramm was still in the living room?"

"N-no—he didn't say anything about that."

"Did you hear anything on the top floor? Anything like a revolver going off?"

"No, I didn't hear anything. I swear it!"

She was so white in the face by now and so hysterical that Nick dared not press her further. In the light of what he had just learned, he was afraid he had already put her through too much. She jumped with fear as he reached for his hat, and he closed his eyes, sickened by the memory of his own brutality. "Please forgive me, Bettina." He looked at her helplessly. "I didn't mean to hurt you. I didn't mean to frighten you."

"It was my fault," she said without tears. Her voice was lower, deeper, almost the voice of a woman. When he was at the door, she spoke again. "I'm sorry I made a pass at you, Nick. Please forget I did that."

"I don't know what you mean," Nick said. "You must have imagined it." He stayed another moment. "You're not a misfit or a mental case, Bettina. Lots of people break down when they're young. They get over it."

"Do they?" She smiled wanly. "Maybe I will too."

He left her at the kitchen table and went down the stairs. Outside he stood some minutes on the brownstone stoop gazing at the street with unseeing eyes. The girl, pathetic as she was, did not stay long in his thoughts; he was too absorbed in what she had told him.

Apparently there had been quite a scene that night between Stramm and Keith Tilden, a scene arising, it would seem, out of an antagonism that stretched back into the past. What had the girl said just now? Stramm had tried to play the heavy father around the house. Nick could easily picture it. The weak, vain man, stupidly trying to assert his authority—the surly boy hating him, judging him with the scornful, unforgiving eyes of youth. And Letty, caught between them, short-tempered, impatient, unable to give up the slavish adoration of her lover, weakly trying to reconcile what could not be reconciled, Letty, never quite choosing between her lover and her son. . . .

Thunder rumbled somewhere and the sky grew darker. Nick turned up his collar and went out into the street. He found Jackman's telephone number in a public booth at the corner. Both his residence and office were listed at the same Park Avenue address, but Nick got no answer at one of the numbers and a busy signal when he tried the other. It seemed a waste of time to call. He hailed a taxi and gave the driver the address.

The wind was beginning to blow up hard again on the way uptown. By the time he got out on Park Avenue, a fierce drenching rain was once again coming down.

Shock

Three kinds of shock.
The shock of heaven, which is thunder.
The shock of fate.
The shock of the heart.

The bronze plaque on the wall bore the legend Ralph Jackman, M.D. Nick rang, rang again, then remembered it was Saturday and Jackman would not have office hours. He should not have come to this side door on the street but to the main entrance on the avenue. He was about to make a run for the corner when the door at which he stood was suddenly flung wide. Midge Jackman, her eyes dazed, her hair and clothing in disarray, stood facing him in the doorway.

Nick stared back at her with a sense of total confusion. "Nick!" she said with a gasp, "why have you come? Who sent you?"

He stammered out something, but before he had finished she was trying to shut the door on him. "You can't come in!" she called out. "Go away. Something terrible has happened."

Nick put his shoulder against the door. "Hold it, Midge," he exclaimed grimly. "What's going on?"

"For God's sake, go away!" she repeated desperately. "You mustn't be found here. Police are coming!"

"*Police?*"

"Yes! Yes!" She was still trying to shut the door, but Nick, resisting steadily, pushed his way into a narrow vestibule. "Now what is all this?" he demanded breathlessly. "What are you doing here?"

She made an effort to collect herself. "It was Ralph," she explained. "He seemed terrified when I called him. He begged me to come, so I did. I thought it was all crazy nonsense, but when I came in, when I came in—he was lying there—" She collapsed against Nick's shoulder, weeping hysterically. "Nick, he's been shot!" she wailed. "I think he's going to die!"

"*What?* Where is he?"

"You can't see him now. I told you. They'll be here any minute!"

"*Where is he?*" He repeated it savagely.

She ran a hand through her hair. "All right. But for God's sake, be quick!"

She hurried him through a maze of office corridors, and he followed her through a thick double door into a splendid room with a gallery on three sides. A red velvet staircase led to these upper regions of the Jackman apartment. The doctor lay at the foot of the staircase. His eyes were open and alert. He had flung out one hand over the carpet. The other clutched at a small brownish stain on his shirtfront. He was breathing in long strange sighs.

"How long has he been like this?"

"I don't know. I can't make him speak. I called Emergency, and they warned me not to move him."

Nick bent over the frail form in the dapper tan suit. "Dr. Jackman!" he called urgently. "Dr. Jackman! Who did this to you?"

The doctor slowly turned his eyes. His entire will was concentrated on remaining alive. He had none of it to spare.

Nick tried again. "Who was it? Can you say the name?" The eyes rolled again. A sound between a sob and a cackle issued from behind the moustache. "Make him get awa-a-ay!"

It was useless. The man was afraid to speak.

Nick, straightening up, found that Midge was no longer beside him. Had she gone mad? She was walking up and down the staircase, searching for something. "Where is it?" she muttered. "It was here. I *saw* it here!" Nick stared. She was not distraught, she was not frightened. She was furiously *angry!* The faint wail of a siren was coming down the street. She turned on Nick in wrath. "I told you not to do this!" she cried. "Now they'll find you!" She stopped him as he blindly turned. "Not that way," she said with furious scorn. "The side door!"

Nick found himself hurried back through narrow halls and practically thrust out into the street. "You haven't been here!" Midge whispered fiercely. "You know nothing about this. Nothing! Do you understand?"

He was glad enough to have anyone direct him. He had taken a terrible chance, and knew it now by the hammering in his chest. He was barely down the block when the ambulance, sounding its siren, came to a screaming halt around the corner.

He hurried eastward, fleeing like some criminal, his thoughts in confusion. Was he the hunter now, or the hunted? On Third Avenue he caught a taxi and told the driver to take him to a midtown hotel. He dismissed the cab there, walked through the lobby and out again, only to flag down another cab. He was drawing on memories of old thrillers, old movies seen in boyhood.

There wasn't a soul on Washington Street when the cab drove off, and the rain was coming down hard. Once again he stood motionless, staring up at the blind facade of the empty house. Some instinct made him reject the areaway this time. Mounting the stoop, he entered with his key by the splendid white door with its great gilt knocker. "Is anybody there?" he cried, standing in the empty hall. And again, "Is anybody there?"

Nobody answered, but quick footsteps ran along the landing and a door slammed shut.

Nick went up the stair, shouting, *"Keith! Keith Tilden!"* in a voice to wake the dead and damned. He burst open the bedroom door.

A woman was standing at the far end of the room. A terrible woman in a dark hat and a coat still dripping with the rain. "Why, Nick!" she called in gay surprise, "was that *you* shouting like that on the stairs?"

Nick stared back. He was not having a bad dream. It was Letty standing there across the room. She had thrust one gloved hand against her side in a clumsy last-minute effort to hide something she was holding—something hideously plain to see.

"Why don't you put it back?" Nick inquired politely.

She seemed not to understand.

"It's what you came for, isn't it?" Nick said. "To put it back?"

"Yes! Of course!" She seemed to wonder how she had come by such a thing. "Yes! I must do that!" Turning, she opened the drawer of the cherrywood table, closed it firmly, and swung about to face him again. "There!" she exclaimed with a gay laugh. *"That's* done!"

Nick walked out, found his way down the stair, and sat down somewhere in the hall below, without knowing how he got there. He was sick to his soul with what he had seen.

For a long time there was absolute silence on the floor above. But at last he heard her footsteps coming down the stair. She stood before him, very pale, but without that awful fixed smile. "You scared me, calling out for Keith like that, Nick!" she said with a nervous laugh. And then, "What's wrong? Were you surprised to find me up there in Bill's room? I only went there because I wanted to—to—" Her words died away in a long silence.

"What are you doing in New York?" Nick finally asked.

"I drove in with Midge." A pause. "Ralph seemed upset when Midge called him. She thought she'd better come in. I decided I would come with her—because—"

"The wound is in his chest," Nick said.

97

"What?" Her breath caught.

"Dr. Jackman. I just saw him. The wound is in his chest. I think he's going to die."

A convulsive movement escaped her. She seemed to collapse, to grow smaller, to shrink. "Oh, God!" Her voice was hoarse, unrecognizable. "Don't say he's going to die. He's hurt, but he's not going to die!"

"Isn't it better for you if he does?" Nick inquired politely.

"Better?" She repeated it mechanically. Turning away, she fumbled convulsively in her bag. She looked suddenly haggard, older than her years. "Better!" she muttered. "Yes! How clever of you to see it, Nick." She straightened up, shut the bag with a snap. She had somehow pulled herself together. "Yes!" she said again. "What's done is done." She faced him, all the dreadful coquetry gone. "I must leave now," she said coldly. "I have no more time. You understand, of course, that nobody must know I've been here."

As he stared, she repeated it with impatience, even with insolence. "I must go! I have an opening tonight."

"How did you come in?"

"We took the car. Midge drove."

"Where is it now?"

"Down the street."

He got up, found his hat and left the house with her.

The Mercedes was parked several houses down. Letty was some time trying to get the door unlocked. She was shivering, beginning to show the strain of what she had been through.

"Can you drive?" Nick asked her.

She shook her head. A mute negative.

"Give me the keys." Impatiently, "Give me the keys! It's clear you'll never make it by yourself."

She gave him the keys. Nick unlocked the door, got in and took the wheel. She went around the other side, and he leaned over and released the door for her.

The trip took two hours, and they spoke only twice. The first exchange was brief. Letty was shivering again, and Nick stopped the car, took off his raincoat, and told her to put it around her shoulders. After this they drove on silently. At the end of an hour he pulled up at a roadside diner and got out and came back with hamburger sandwiches and containers of coffee. They both fell on the food with famished greed. When they finished, Nick did not start the car again but remained in thought. After a while he asked Letty who in New Haven knew she had gone to New York that day.

"Nobody knew," Letty said.

"I see." He took that in and said, "And what's the story?"

"The story?"

"You left Midge over on Park Avenue to deal with the police," Nick reminded her pointedly. "You must have fixed up some kind of scenario between you."

She flushed faintly. "Midge is supposed to have come in by train."

"And what are you 'supposed' to have done?"

He could not keep a cutting contempt out of it, and she sat in silence, her eyes lowered.

Nick let a moment pass and said, "What time did the two of you leave New Haven?"

"Three o'clock. When the rehearsal ended."

He glanced at his wristwatch. "We won't get back before eight. How are you going to account for those five hours?"

"How can I account for them? I'll have to say I was in my hotel room."

"For five hours?"

"There's nothing else I *can* say."

"Couldn't you have gone shopping? Or to a movie?"

"Someone would have seen me, recognized me."

"Suppose a call came in for you? You were in your room. Why didn't you answer?"

"I don't know," she returned desperately. "I didn't hear it. I was nervous! I took a tranquilizer. I was asleep. I didn't care. For God's sake, can't this wait? The curtain goes up at eight fifteen!"

"They're going to question you," he pointed out coldly.

99

"I won't answer!" she broke out. "I'll refuse! I can't go through with it!"

"You *must* go through with it!" he exclaimed with anger.

"Why?" she countered. "Can't I be sick? Can't I get out of it?"

"No, you can't."

She subsided.

He waited a little again. "Don't the clerks at the desk know when people are in their rooms and when they're not?"

"I don't think they do. I keep my room key with me. There's an automatic elevator. It's a big crowded lobby. We've been there a week now, coming and going. I don't think they pay attention anymore."

A bitter smile twisted his lips. "I'm glad you've thought everything out so well, Letty. You're usually so vague—so careless."

After this he started the car, and they did not speak again. Nick was trying to make time on the road. Letty, exhausted, lay back with her eyes shut. She was so still and white that at one point he thought she had fainted. But she murmured faintly, "Just get me there!"

He pressed on grimly. He would never understand these people. All she cared about now was getting to New Haven in time for the curtain!

By seven the rain had stopped. Half an hour more, and they were driving under cool blue evening skies. At one minute past eight the marquee of the Shubert Theatre came into view. LORETTE HARRIS in THE MASQUERS. It was spelled out in electric lights. A well dressed first-night crowd was already moving through the doors into the theater. The city looked festive, all its lights gleaming. A perfect night. A great night for the opening.

Nick pulled the car up at the stage entrance. Letty set herself to rights with a few touches and got out. Every trace of fatigue and weakness had left her. She moved toward the stage entrance swiftly, purposefully, her heels clicking a grim, determined rhythm on the pavement.

Nick stayed with her as she hurried through the alley, through the door and onto the stage where, behind the asbestos curtain, the huge muffled hum of the audience could already be heard. Actors and stagehands moved about in a shadowy semidarkness, and as she passed, someone called her name in a startled whisper. Jim Benson, the stage manager, visibly sagged with relief when he saw her. "Miss Harris! Thank the Lord you're here!" he gasped.

"Hold the curtain a few minutes, will you, Jim?" She threw it quietly over her shoulder as she hurried on.

As she moved across the stage a dressing-room door swung open. Bacchus, his hand on the knob, was talking to people in the room. ". . . and make the announcement," Bacchus was saying. "If Clarissa can go through with it, we won't cancel. But there's no time left."

A worried murmur answered him. Inside the room, the director, the playwright and several actors were gathered in a tense knot, all eyes on Letty's understudy, Clarissa Howe. Standing in the center of the room, her body rigid with fear, the standby was being hooked into a scarlet gown by an elderly woman in a dark dress and black apron.

It was this woman who first saw Letty through the open door and who quietly said, "It's all right, Mr. Bacchus. Miss Harris is here now."

Preponderance of the Great

The weight of the load is too great.
The ridgepole that holds up the roof sags.
Disaster.

Letty wasted no time on explanations. She stepped behind a screen, where she removed her hat and dress, reappearing immediately in a pale, short-sleeved cotton wrapper. Seating herself at her dressing table, she began quickly and efficiently working cold cream into her face. She paused once to glance at the others and say in a curt tone, "Please let me dress."

Her arrival released a quiet explosion of activity. Joe Lechay came out into the corridor, looked at Nick with no glimmer of recognition, and set off on some urgent business of his own. Clarissa Howe, stripped of the scarlet gown, was hustled away to her own room. There were tears in her eyes, but whether they were of relief or disappointment, no one could say. Jim Benson, the stage manager, went up and down the corridor, knocking on dressing-room doors and calling out that the curtain would go up in ten minutes. Actors hurried by, pausing to talk excitedly. Lilo, in a rag of a dress, turned and gave Nick a long disconcerting stare. And a clown with a white face came up to him, asked an excited question, but waved his arms and went away without an answer.

Bacchus, last to emerge from Letty's room, found Nick waiting just outside the door. The two men hung eye to eye.

"I want to talk to you," Nick said.

"This is hardly the moment."

"I think we have to talk."

"Perhaps we do. But not now."

For the second time that day Nick felt a rage that seemed to explode somewhere at the back of his skull. As Bacchus attempted to pass on, Nick stopped him with a hand on his shoulder. "Who turned on the lights in the court that night, Bill?" he asked him in a low hard tone.

"The lights? What—?" Bacchus was suddenly wary.

"You staged that scene," Nick told him softly. "A corpse in the backyard. Beautifully lit. I saw it as soon as I walked in. That was the idea, wasn't it? That I was to see it?"

"Please let me pass," Bacchus said. His face was full of menace.

Nick did not stop him, but said in a low, distinct voice, "Ralph Jackman was shot today."

It turned Bacchus around as if on a pivot. Words choked at the back of his throat.

"He was shot," Nick repeated. "In the chest. I think he's dying."

"You're trying to trick me!" Bacchus whispered. His eyes were bulging apoplectically. "Trying to trick me with a lie. *Trick me?*" For a crazy instant his fist went back. But even as he threatened to strike, his terror-stricken eyes were begging for mercy.

Nick said in a low, harsh voice, "Why in hell did you let her

103

go in today? Didn't you know something like this would happen?"

Bacchus walked away without answering. After a few steps he stumbled and would have lost his balance if Jim Benson had not caught him by the arm. Straightening up, he pointed to Nick and gasped out, "Send him out front! Get him away—away from the actors." His spasmodic breathing and contorted face made a frightened silence in the corridor.

The stage manager, badly worried, asked Nick if he would like to see the play. Nick hardly understood what he said but followed him across the stage to a steel fire door. This opened into a vast, half-darkened cavern full of the rustle and stirring of the audience. Nick had passed, without transition, into the hall of the theater. And nothing that day seemed to him so dreamlike, so unreal, as those orderly rows of pleasant people who had come to see a play.

He found a seat somewhere at the back of the house and sank into it, grateful for the surrounding darkness. The blood was still pounding in his temples from that terrible encounter with Bacchus.

He had no sooner seated himself than the murmurs and whispers in the audience died into a silence. This was broken by the pounding beat of a drum. On this the curtain rose.

Lilo strode around the stage in a wide half circle, her dress barely covering a superb body. A white-faced clown beat out a rhythm for her on a drum. The clown, Nick realized, was Arnaboldi, whom he had failed to recognize in the corridor. A round of spontaneous applause broke out for the William Bacchus set—an eerie no-man's-land with muffled gunfire in the distance.

All through the scene with the three townsmen Nick waited tensely, knowing Letty was soon to appear. Her offstage "Hey, clown!" speech sent a wave of expectation through the house. A moment later she walked on. It was her first public appearance in five years. She looked extraordinary in the scarlet dress. Her personal trouble lent a note of drama to the moment. There was something of courage in her being there at all, and her entrance met with a ringing, prolonged crash of applause.

She played her first scene well, but halfway through some dialogue with the Showmaster she stumbled over her lines. Instead of covering, she stopped dead and, after a silence, went back to the beginning of her speech. A whisper like a vast sigh passed through the audience. But Letty played on with renewed authority, and her lapse was forgotten.

Nick, watching her, marveled at her strength. The play, with its themes of betrayal and murder, was an assault on every nerve in his body. He did not understand an audience that took it so quietly, indeed were pleasantly entertained by it. Murder, for these people, was something in the evening papers—war an event in which other people died. For Nick, such things had become all too real. At times he confused what he saw on the stage with scenes he had lived through that day. Instead of the actors he saw Jackman at the foot of the stair. The Letty in the play was replaced by a Letty smiling at him falsely, a gun in her hand.

Lost in these dark thoughts, the action on stage came to Nick in disconnected snatches: the entrance of a gigantic, half-naked figure—Samuel Lucas as the Slave. Lilo, delivering a brutally effective monologue about her childhood years as a soldier's whore. Now and again bits of dialogue reached him.

THE GIRL: The old people say there was a Time Before—a time when there was no war.

SHOWMASTER: They're dreaming. There was no such time.

Another bit—this time the Clown and the Slave:

CLOWN: It will all be over soon. The Enemy is winning—everyone knows it.

SLAVE (laughs): It will be bad if they win.

CLOWN (frightened): Why? What will they do?

SLAVE (laughs): It will be bad. The lucky ones will be dead.

The scene shifted. A tavern now. Letty, in the scarlet dress, danced with the Enemy Captain. There was some talk about "the Countess"—an old woman who, with a remnant of her guard, kept the Enemy out. The curtain came down on the first act as Letty and the Showmaster agreed to sell out the town in return for the murder of the Slave.

As soon as the lights went up, Nick left his seat and found his way backstage. Men here were shifting scenery for the second half of the play. Confused by the shouting and movement, Nick lost his way. Retracing his steps, he came on Clayton Collier and Lilo talking in a passageway. Collier seemed startled to see him. Lilo gave him another long queer look. There was tension in the air, and Nick wondered just what was up back here.

A moment later, as he came onto the darkened stage, Arnaboldi seized him by the arms. "Armisen?" he whispered. "Have you heard? Something happened to Jackman today. Something happened to him there in New York."

Sweat came out on Nick's forehead. "Did Bacchus tell you that?"

"No! No! Don't you know what's going on?" He looked about and his voice sank to a frightened whisper. "Police are here! They came backstage! A little while ago."

Although Nick should have expected it, the news hit him like a body blow.

"They waited in the wings until Letty came off. There's something they told her. Something about Keith. I don't know what it was, but she almost fainted."

"Where is she now?"

"Lechay got her into her dressing room. They wanted to go in after her, but Bacchus stood in front of the door and wouldn't let them in." Arnaboldi moistened dry lips. He was shaking from head to foot. "Nick! It is true that something happened today— That something happened to—?"

"Yes, it happened!" Nick answered savagely. "And for all I know, you were *there* when it happened!"

Arnaboldi fell back as though he had been struck. "You don't mean that, Nick!" he stammered out in consternation. "You can't mean it! Nick! You've been our friend!"

Nick's eyes were ice. He said, "Don't bank on my friendship, Leo, and I won't bank on yours!" He went past him and on, across the stage.

They were standing not far from Letty's door. The uniformed younger officer was probably part of the New Haven police force. The balding middle-aged man beside him was most likely a detective. The third man was Lieutenant Goodine of Manhattan South Homicide. The three of them were in conference with Bacchus and Joe Lechay. Bacchus stood by iron-faced and let Lechay do the talking. Lechay, looking pale and determined, was insisting that questions be deferred until after the performance.

"A man has been shot," Goodine pointed out. "He may already have died."

"That may be so," Lechay replied. "My own responsibilities remain." A hard note came into his voice. "Considerable investment has been made in this play, gentlemen. I don't want to appear high-handed in this matter, but I cannot allow you to disrupt our performance tonight."

A wrangle followed. Lechay offered to call a general meeting with Goodine and the other officers present and free to ask any questions they chose. Goodine bargained. He was willing to wait until the performance was over, but wanted to interview each actor singly and alone. Lechay blew up at that, and refused to put his cast through any such ordeal. Goodine shrugged, and with a certain contempt, said he could not force the company to cooperate. After learning where the actors could be reached, the three men left the theater.

Bacchus turned away wordlessly. Lechay wiped his forehead with a handkerchief and for the first time glanced at Nick. "Do you want to go in and see her?" he asked quietly.

Nick said he would. Lechay rapped sharply and with authority at her dressing-room door, calling out his own name as he did so.

The elderly dresser opened it for them. Letty was seated at the mirror, her body turned sharply toward the door. As soon as she caught sight of them she called out hysterically, "Joe! Get Harold Lasher! Get him now! They've arrested Keith!"

"Shut the door!" Lechay said sharply. Nick closed it behind him. So that was the news the police had given her on the stage!

Letty said again, "Lasher has to go down there. He has to get Keith out!"

"I've already called him," Lechay said. "He'll get back to us as soon as we reach him." He mopped his forehead. "Keith hasn't been arrested, Letty. I wish you'd try to be a little more calm about this. He's only been held for questioning. As soon as they realize he had nothing to do with it, they'll let him go."

"Yes. Yes." She looked about with distracted eyes. "Lasher must get him out!"

"I'll call him again. Will that make you feel better?"

"Yes, Joe, dear. Do that." She subsided. Her tone had grown lifeless.

Lechay lingered, taking her in with worried eyes. "How do you feel? Can you go through the second half?"

"Yes, I can do it."

"All right. I'll go now and make the call." A pause. "Would you like Mr. Armisen to stay here with you?"

She looked up at Nick, but her eyes had gone dead, and she looked away again, shaking her head. Her "No" was barely audible.

"Well—" Lechay hesitated. "Mrs. Wood will look after you, I'm sure."

"That I will," the dresser quietly assured him.

The two men walked out into the corridor. Lechay went off, a much beset man. Nick found his way to the stage door and left the theater.

A cool breeze was blowing through the alley outside the stage door, and he lingered, wanting the freshness of it on his face. It was a bit of a shock that Letty had not wanted him in her room. More than any event that day, it seemed to mark the end of something.

The crowd was moving back into the theater for the second act as he came around the corner. Not far from the marquee with its electric sign a tall figure in a gray gabardine coat stood quietly back against the building.

"Good evening, Mr. Armisen," said Lieutenant Goodine.

"Good evening."

"Do you mind if we talk a little?"

"Talk about what?" Nick's tone was sharp.

"There was a shooting today in New York. You may have heard about that."

"Only what they told me inside." Then, since it seemed necessary to add something, "Exactly what did happen?"

Goodine held out a pack of cigarettes. Nick declined, and Goodine selected a cigarette for himself, taking his time about it. "Have you been in New Haven long, Mr. Armisen?" he inquired pleasantly.

"I came out tonight for the opening."

"By train?"

This was not safe ground. Since he wanted neither to confirm nor to deny this, Nick did not answer.

Goodine was busy with his cigarette. "Mrs. Tilden probably picked you up at the station."

Nick was pleasant-faced but silent.

"You and Mrs. Tilden have become rather good friends lately," Goodine observed.

"Pardon me, Lieutenant," Nick interrupted. "Is that really part of your concern?"

"Perhaps not." He lit his cigarette, shielding the flame with a cupped hand. "According to your statement, Mr. Armisen, you were at a party given by a friend on the night Kenneth Stramm died."

So it had finally come! Nick braced himself.

"From what you told us," Goodine went on, "you remained at this party until four o'clock that morning. But we have information now that you left at least two hours before." Goodine waited. "Do you happen to remember where you spent those two hours?"

After thinking a little Nick said, "Why should my whereabouts that night be important to you, Lieutenant? Are you implying that I had something to do with what happened to Mr. Stramm?"

"If you did, we'll find a way to prove it. We're very patient men, Mr. Armisen. You'd be smarter to cooperate with us and tell us what we need to know."

109

It occurred to Nick that he could rid himself of this man simply by telling him the truth. The momentary temptation passed. He would not be quits with Goodine if he told the truth. He would have become Goodine's ally.

"I'm not sure I like the interrogation," he said. "If you think I had something to do with Mr. Stramm's death, take me in as a suspect. Go ahead! Arrest me! Let's see if you can make it stick!"

"I wouldn't take that tone, Mr. Armisen!"

"Go to hell!" Nick said recklessly. "I'll take any tone I like!" And walking past Goodine, he mingled with the crowd in the lobby and passed inside the theater.

An uproar of applause broke out as he entered. The curtain had just gone up on the second half of the play, and the audience was responding to a scenic masterpiece. Nick stared at the stage. There it was, come to life—the tall windows with their tattered red hangings, the threadbare moth-eaten carpets, the broken throne leaning crazily on its three legs—the marvelous little "Room in a Ruined Castle" rose up before him as a stunning theatrical reality.

Through the salvos of applause Nick seemed to hear Bacchus again. *Everybody wanted to see the set. We all rode up to the top floor.* (And right there, Nick told himself, I felt something was wrong with the whole story!) With the life-size set before him on the stage, Nick once again had that teasing sensation of an idea rising to the surface of his mind, an idea that almost broke through. . . .

But the scene had begun. Letty, in the dark dress of a servant, stood center stage with the Clown and the Showmaster. There was something they wanted Letty to do. She was backing off fearfully, asking if there was not some other way.

The Showmaster urges her on impatiently, assures her the whole thing will take no more than a minute.

The two men hide. Sarah Hall enters as the Old Countess. She is a corpselike figure covered from chin to toes in a shroudlike gown of white lace.

110

LETTY *(coming forward)*: Madame—Madame!

COUNTESS: Yes? *(frightened)* What do you want? Who are you?

The two men fall on her and drag her off. A choked muffled cry, then a silence. The Clown and Showmaster reappear, bringing the dress, which trails along the floor. Letty draws back as she sees it.

SHOWMASTER: It's over! All you have to do is put the dress on, go to the window and give the surrender signal. Hurry! Do as I say! *(holds out the dress)*

LETTY: This too? All for the show? To ride around on the empty bombed-out roads with the show?

SHOWMASTER: It's the way we live.

LETTY: Can't we live another way?

SHOWMASTER: We don't know how. Go on. Put the dress on. She won't mind, since she's dead. *(hurrying her)* Go on! It's for our love too. *(tries to embrace her)*

LETTY: But—do we still love each other?

SHOWMASTER *(gloomily)*: Enough for this.

LETTY: Yes—for this.

It was Letty's most important scene, but she was going through it like a sleepwalker. Twice she missed her cue, and the second time, Collier could actually be heard throwing her the lines. Even then she did not speak, but remained silent and motionless until a loud murmur of dismay ran right through the audience.

She had a good scene afterward with the Enemy Captain, but though she went through it creditably, the impression could no longer be recovered. What should have been the high point of her performance had ended with a few scattered handclaps.

The lights went down. The set shifted. Once again, the no-man's-land of the first scene. The Slave lies murdered on the road. Letty, Arnaboldi and the Showmaster are machine-gunned as they try to cross the enemy lines. Only Lilo, the Girl, is alive among the bodies of the dead.

The Girl, who has loathed them all her life, runs from one to the other, weeping, pleading with each of them to wake, to live again. "Oh, they are dead!" she finally cries out in despair. "All of them! I am alone. Where shall I go?"

Gunfire is heard. The Girl, terrified, runs here, there, her figure finally disappearing in a kind of mist at the back of the stage. Only her cry echoes back: "Alone—alone!" Cannon speak. Bombs flare in the distance. The curtain falls.

The play had ended on a genuinely moving antiwar statement, and there was a tremendous response from the house. Each of the players received ringing appreciative applause. The Slave was enthusiastically greeted, as were Collier, the Enemy Captain and Arnaboldi. But the applause swelled to a thunderous ovation as Lilo came forward for her bow. Again and again, her name was called out while the whole theater rocked with bravos.

Letty was generously received. She was the star, and her failures were forgiven. But the audience wanted Lilo, and once again thunder shook the house as the young actress once again came forward.

She had scored an outstanding triumph, and every critic would say so. Letty wasn't even in it. It was Lilo's night.

Splitting Apart

The forces of darkness
splinter the light.
Splitting Apart means ruin.

"I think the entire cast is aware," Joe Lechay said, "that an unfortunate incident took place tonight. Police were in the house, and certain members of the company were questioned while the performance was going on. I called this meeting because the cast is entitled to know why this happened."

The cast was assembled in the Green Room of the theater. Chairs here were limited, and a number of actors were standing at the back. Nick, at Lechay's request, was among them. Bacchus, seated not far away, never glanced in his direction. And Arnaboldi, looking close to collapse, was also careful to avoid his eyes. Letty had remained in her dressing room. She was the only member of the cast not present at the meeting.

Lechay continued. "While I've been assured that none of us is under suspicion, I must inform you that a crime, in fact, has been committed. Dr. Jackman, whom some of us have known a number of years, was mysteriously shot in New York today."

Since the entire cast already knew this, nobody offered a comment.

Lechay went on. "The police, who did not want to disrupt our opening, were decent enough to leave. But they do want to ask some questions, and some of us, possibly all of us, may be asked to go down to headquarters tomorrow." A murmur of dismay greeted this. Lechay raised his voice over it. "We are making every effort to contact Equity about this," he told the cast. "And I have already spoken to Harold Lasher, my own attorney. I understand from Lasher that no one here is legally bound to answer questions unless he chooses to do so. There is no reason why any of us should *not* comply, but we are within our rights if we refuse." He waved a hand and said, "That's all. The floor is open."

"Is Jackman dead?" a voice presently asked.

"He is in the intensive care unit of New York Hospital. I understand his condition is critical."

"Well, of course we are terribly shocked and sorry for the poor man." Clayton Collier was drawing his words out in a consciously leisurely, detached way. "What I can't see, Joe, is why the police think *we* can be of any help to them in this business!"

A resentful murmur went up. Sarah Hall burst out vehemently, "Clayton is right! What have *we* to do with their beastly murders?"

"Well, we do have to face facts, Sarah," Sam Lucas reminded her mildly. "Any one of us might have taken a flyer into New York today, done the job and—scooted back!"

"What nonsense!" She was scornful. "We were rehearsing right here all morning—" But she stopped there, aware of a flaw in her argument.

"Less than two hours to New York," a voice commented.

"Rehearsal ended before three," another said.

"Time enough!" A third laconic comment.

"That does seem to be the way they're looking at it," Lechay agreed. "However, I'm sure we can all easily account for our movements today."

His words sank into a silence. Everyone was thinking of Letty's last-minute arrival that night, but nobody wanted to be the one to mention it. A voice from the back presently asked why Miss Harris was not at the meeting.

"Miss Harris," Lechay answered coldly, "behaved with considerable heroism tonight. She received extremely bad news and in spite of it, went on with the performance." He added in a more careless tone, addressing only Bacchus, "I gather Letty was resting in her hotel room most of the afternoon."

"Quite right."

"Still"—Lechay looked about the room—"still, it's possible someone might have caught a glimpse of her at one point or another."

This brought the longest silence yet. At last a voice at the back spoke up, saying, "I saw Lorette today."

Every head turned. It was Lilo.

"Where was it you saw her, Lilo?" Lechay asked, clearly much relieved.

"At the hotel. Her room is a few doors down from mine. I was out of cigarettes. I knocked at her door and asked if she had any."

Several cynical glances were exchanged at this. Everyone knew Lilo's feeling about the star; she had made no secret of it. The entire rehearsal period had been marked by the tension between the two actresses. The intimacy of shared cigarettes was patently absurd, and the air fairly hummed with disbelief. Apparently the girl felt it herself, for she came out again in a shockingly strident voice. "All right! She's been hogging my scenes. I was sick of it, and I walked in and told her so!"

Nick was completely at sea. Letty had left for New York immediately after the rehearsal. At no point after that had she been in her hotel room. The girl was lying. The curious thing was that everyone else seemed to understand. An odd quiet settled over the room. The actors seemed to be watching, waiting to see if she could pull it off—make her story stick.

Lechay said carefully, "How long were you together? Can you remember?"

"Ten minutes." She looked tough and defiant. She knew nobody believed her.

"Do you happen to remember what time it was?"

"I didn't time it!" She cast a surreptitious look about her, something like hatred in her eyes. She might almost have said it aloud: "*I'm giving you what you need, damn you! Isn't that enough?*"

"Would you be willing to make a statement about this to the police?"

She shrugged. "Why shouldn't I?"

Since there were no questions, Lechay closed the meeting. The actors gathered in groups, discussing the situation; others left the theater to talk elsewhere. Lilo walked out quickly and alone.

Nick hung about the hall outside until Bacchus and Arnaboldi left. When Lechay came out, Nick asked how Jackman was.

"I just heard from Lasher," the director replied in a low voice. "It's all over."

"Dead?"

"At ten thirty."

"Does Letty know?"

"I told her just before the meeting."

Nick took this in and said he would get Letty back to the hotel.

Minutes later, walking into her dressing room, Nick came face to face with Lilo leaving it. Lilo had naturally lost no time hurrying back here. It was vital that her story tally with whatever story Letty would tell. Nick wondered what their conversation had been just before he entered. The girl swung past him with another of her insolent stares. In some way Nick seemed to be included in her bitterness about the star of the play. Nick thought it impertinent of her to have feelings about him at all. He turned away with a blank face.

If Letty was surprised that help had come from this unexpected quarter, she gave no sign of it. She was sitting motionless at her dressing table, still in the dark servant's dress of the second act.

"Why didn't you come to the meeting?" Nick asked her.

"The meeting?"

"You shouldn't have stayed away. It made a bad impression."

She did not answer. She seemed not to understand.

"Get dressed," Nick said. "I'll take you back to the hotel."

A small black Ford tagged behind them all the way. Nick got a look at the driver when the car pulled up alongside at a red light. It was the balding middle-aged plainclothesman Nick had seen in the theater. By the time Nick booked a room, he was settling down in the lobby with a newspaper. Clearly, he was prepared to sit there all night.

"You shot him," Nick said. "You shot him, or you were there when someone else did it."

"I didn't shoot him," Letty said. "We found him at the foot of the staircase."

"He was beginning to weaken." Nick was figuring it out as he spoke. "The I Ching letter didn't work so well. Instead of shutting his mouth, it sent him into panic. He was getting ready to spill everything he knew. So you killed him."

"No, Nick. I didn't kill him."

"You and Midge drove in and got the gun. Then you went uptown and took care of Jackman. You left Midge uptown, drove back to Washington Street, and put the gun back in the drawer."

"No, Nick," Letty said again. "No. It wasn't like that."

They were in her room at the hotel. She had not removed her makeup, and the chalk white face of the last act was startling against the dark coronet of her hair.

"Bacchus and Arnaboldi aren't out of this," Nick pursued. "They could have driven in with you and taken a train back to New Haven."

"They didn't drive in with us," Letty said. "It was just myself and Midge."

Nick laughed. "Bacchus and Arnaboldi stayed here in New Haven. You and Midge found him already shot. There's no one left who could have done it but Keith."

"You're wrong! You're wrong, Nick!"

"Then who? Somebody pointed that gun. Somebody pulled the trigger and killed that man!"

"Don't do this to me, Nick. Not tonight." She began to cry. "Get the police. I'll confess. I killed him. I killed them all!"

"Oh, don't give me any of your *acting!*" Nick said with a white flash of anger.

"My acting!" she said slowly. "My acting."

He was questioning her further when the phone rang and she was across the room in a flash. It was Lasher, finally, with news. After several tense controlled questions Letty uttered a harsh gasping exclamation and turning away, said to Nick, "Keith has been arrested! He's going to be arraigned Monday morning." A hoarse dry sob escaped her. The phone slipped out of her nerveless hand, and she fell into a chair. Nick picked up the receiver and asked Lasher to give him the facts. "My God, Armisen, tell Letty she's got to get hold of herself!" the lawyer exclaimed with feeling.

"What's the situation?" Nick asked. "How do things look?"

"Not good," Lasher admitted. "They've located one of the doormen. The one who was on duty this afternoon. He says Keith went into Jackman's apartment at four o'clock today."

"Could the doorman be mistaken?"

"No chance. Keith has been in and out of that apartment house since he was a kid. Everyone in the building knows him."

"What does Keith say?"

Lasher sighed. "Keith told three stories and backtracked on all of them. What he finally told *me* is this: Jackman called him yesterday and accused him of sending some crazy letter through the mail. Keith denied it. He wanted to come over and see Jackman, but Jackman seemed afraid to see him. Keith was still disturbed about it today, so he called Jackman around noon and insisted again on a meeting. Jackman would only meet him in a

118

public place. They made an appointment at Radio City Music Hall. Keith got there on time, Jackman never showed. After an hour or so, Keith got sick of waiting and went up to his apartment. He says Jackman went into a state of unreasoning fear when he came in, pulled out a gun and backed away up the stairs. Keith followed, trying to take the gun away. The gun went off. Jackman fell headlong to the foot of the stairs. Keith thought he was dead. He panicked and ran out through the side door. Doorman never heard the gun go off. He was outside, flagging down a cab."

Nick was giving this story some hard thought. "How does all that add up, Harold?"

"It's Keith's story. He swears it's true." Lasher didn't sound happy about it.

"What do the police think?"

"Well, the thing's got some bad holes, no matter how you look at it. For one thing, Keith says he left the gun on the staircase. There was no gun at all when the police got there. It doesn't look good that the gun disappeared."

"I see." Nick was digesting it. "How about Midge? Where is she?"

"She's in pretty fair shape, but the police gave her a rough time of it. They had her down there at least four hours. On top of the shock it was a damn hard thing to go through. She's all right now. At least, I hope she is."

"Well, thanks, Harold," Nick said heavily. "Keep in touch."

"I'm glad you're there with Letty, Armisen. Tell her I'll call as soon as I have news."

Nick hung up. It was something to know for sure that it was Keith. But Letty could still have been part of it. She could even have engineered it.

She was prowling restlessly up and down. As soon as Nick got off the phone she said, "Well—what does he say?"

"It seems one of the doormen saw Keith go into Jackman's apartment today."

"Yes—he already told me that." She was prowling again.

"They can't keep Keith locked up this way until Monday morning. Think of what he's going through."

"They're certainly going to hold him," Nick said bluntly. "He admits he was in that apartment."

"But someone's got to get him out!" she repeated angrily. "They do things to people! They beat them—torture them!"

Sergeant Shellman's image flashed into Nick's mind, but he answered dryly, "Not when they have such expensive lawyers."

"Oh, you just don't care!" Letty cried hysterically. "You've never cared about Keith. Never!"

"It seems to me I've cared enough about both of you," Nick retorted with anger. "My own neck isn't safe, in case you want to know. I didn't have to lie to the police to protect your son. I didn't have to bring you here. I don't know why in hell I *did* bring you here. I could be living my own sweet life in New York, and to hell with both of you!"

She covered her eyes with one hand, sighing. "You've been decency itself—I know that. You're trying to help me. But all this—it's not what I need, not what I need at all."

"It's hard to give you all you need!" he remarked.

"Is it? I need you to be a little kind, Nick. What a fool I am! I need you to love me."

He was silent. He couldn't give her what was dead and gone in his heart.

After a pause she said conversationally, "Kenneth. He's the one I miss. Kenneth would have stuck by me. He wouldn't have thrown me over. No matter what I'd done."

Nick said sardonically, "I'm sorry for your loss."

"Oh, yes, he was a fool. He was stupid with Keith and stupid with me. But he wasn't cold. He wasn't inhuman."

"Meaning that I am?" Nick laughed shortly. "Well, you're not the first woman to say so. So maybe it's true."

"What are we to do?" She seemed to be appealing for an answer to everything—all of life.

"There's nothing to do," he told her. "We'd better get some

sleep." He walked into the bedroom, took off his jacket and then, methodically, his tie. She followed him.

"Nick." A slight falter came into her voice. "I think it would be better if you—if you went to your own room tonight."

He glanced at her quickly but went on hanging his jacket over the back of a chair. "I'll go in a little while," he told her.

"It's only that I'm so tired," Letty said, trying to explain.

It occurred to Nick with anger that there was a room just down the corridor where he would be more than welcome. The blond girl was his for the asking, he knew that. Yet somehow it was this ruinous woman here that he wanted. They had been apart for a week; they were together in a strange city, a strange room; and as suspicion and anger inevitably receded, he wanted her again with an acute, overriding desire.

She fought him weakly, still trying not to offend. "It's just that I'm so worn out, Nick," she pleaded. "I need to be by myself. Don't you understand?"

"There's nothing so hard about what I'm asking," he argued.

"But you've been at me for hours!" she said, with a flare of anger. "Questioning me. Hating me. I can't take any more. I'm tired. I want to sleep."

He wavered at that. But his own day had been hard, too, and what he wanted was easy enough to give. He saw no reason why anything so simple should be denied him. He said mechanically, "You'll get some sleep. I won't stay long."

"Nick!" she said, "I *can't!*"

"Why not?" He refused to understand. "Why can't you?"

"I don't *want* this!" she stormed.

"*I* want it," he said.

He did not at any point force her, but he insisted, and in the end she let him have his way. The rough embrace, in fact, was brief enough. He had cared for nothing but the release he needed, and there was little pleasure in it even for him.

When it was over he told her in a matter-of-fact way to come to bed. He was aware of having treated her rather badly, but he still could see no real harm in what he had done—certainly

121

nothing to account for that shamed look, that white, averted face.

She was a long time getting ready, and as soon as she lay beside him he switched off the bedside lamp. But there was no hope of sleep. Her silent desolation filled the darkness. He turned at last and asked her sharply what was wrong. She lay with an arm flung over her eyes. "What is it?" he asked again, impatient. It was slowly breaking in on him that, force or not, he had taken her against her will—a thing outside his personal code. It was not a pleasant thought, and it made his tone with her distant and harsh.

After a long time she spoke in the ghost of a whisper: "Oh, God! I just feel so alone!"

It was so faint, such a mere breath, he could pretend he had not heard it at all. He turned away again, not indifferent but feeling he could not help her. He told himself she was strong and would survive it. He told himself he was too tired to think about it now.

He woke some hours later with a broad band of light lying across the floor of the room. She was not beside him, and he was up instantly and at the open bathroom door. She was standing in her nightgown, tinkering with something in the medicine chest. Nick's heart seemed to stop. "What are you doing?" he asked.

She turned, smiling vaguely. "I'm feeling awfully queer, Nick. I think something's wrong with me."

She was burning up as she stood there. He could see the fever in her eyes, smell it on her breath.

"What's this?" He opened her closed hand. She let him take the tiny bottle out of it. "Ralph gave them to me. It's this awful headache. I thought they'd make me sleep."

"Haven't you something else? Something for headache?"

"There should be some aspirin."

"Go back to bed. I'll get it for you."

She obeyed like a child.

He found the aspirin and brought it to her with a glass of water

122

from the bathroom. "Do you think you caught a chill?" he asked her.

"I might have. In the rain."

"Well," he said, "maybe you'll feel better in the morning."

The tablets seemed to help, for she burrowed down into the pillow with a sigh as soon as she had taken them. She was asleep almost instantly. And he, too, slept.

The Estranged

The estrangement does not preclude all agreement.
But it has come about
through an inner condition and
outer circumstances cannot change it.

"I've gone over her thoroughly," the doctor said, "and I can't find anything that accounts for this kind of fever. But something is making it go up that high, and in my opinion we ought to get her over to the hospital and run some tests."

Lechay nodded, looking worried. "I suppose she'd better go in." He turned to Nick. "What do you think?"

Nick said the tests sounded like a good idea.

It was a little before ten in the morning. The three of them were standing around her bed.

"I can get her Thorwald Christianson," the doctor said. "You won't find a better man anywhere. And she'll certainly be better off at the hospital than in this hotel room."

He stood there waiting for them to decide. He was in his early fifties, a solidly built man, comfortably settled with a good family practice.

"How long is this going to take?" Letty demanded resentfully. She turned to Lechay. "What about the performance tonight? What about New York?"

"New York is a long way off." But Lechay was not entirely easy himself. "What do you think, Doctor? We've got two weeks. Will she be on her feet?"

The doctor refused to commit himself. He said the lady was running a high fever, and they had to find out why. He said he was not giving out guarantees. "They may send her home in a day or two," he said. "They may not." He added with a touch of professional testiness, "The sooner we get her in, you know, the sooner we can get her out!"

"Go along, Letty," Lechay advised with a sigh. "Better to miss tonight's performance than miss the New York opening."

She fell back on the pillow, half relieved to give up. "I guess Clarissa will do the job," she said wearily. "God knows she can't mess it up any worse than I did."

The doctor got on the phone then and there and made arrangements about a bed. When this had been settled, Letty asked the men to let her dress and get her things together. Nick was following the other two, but she held him back with a quick tense hand on his arm.

As soon as the door closed, her grip tightened convulsively. "Nick, for God's sake, do something for me!" she begged in a hoarse whisper. Her eyes were dark pools of fear in a face that had gone ghastly pale.

"What is it?" he whispered. Her own fear thumped inside his chest.

She got out of bed, ran across the carpet to the closet and came out again clutching her black handbag. She thrust this at him. "Take it!" she whispered. "Don't let anybody see it. Put it somewhere! Hide it!" She was pleading, babbling. "I'll never ask

125

you to do anything else for me, Nick. I swear it! I swear I'll make it up to you someday."

"But won't you need this?" He was in some bewilderment. "Your money? Your things?"

"Later!" she said fiercely. "Take it! Hide it! Now!"

She was so desperate that he simply took the bag and went off with it. Lechay and the doctor had moved away from her door in order to talk together. Neither of them noticed Nick going down the hall in the other direction.

Nick's room was on the same floor but around a bend in the hallway. As soon as he got inside the door, he began ruthlessly searching the handbag. There was money in a soft cream leather wallet and a checkbook from a New York bank. These he set aside as things she would need immediately. Everything else he tossed on top of the bureau. A gold compact. A matching cigarette case. Keys on an Italian leather ring. A key to her hotel room. A pair of rolled up black suede gloves. Two black scented and initialed handkerchiefs. Two sales receipts from New Haven shops. Sunglasses. Cosmetics. And at the bottom of it all something that glinted. A gun.

Nick did not take it out or touch it. He was trying to understand why she had taken it with her to New Haven. *"Why don't you put it back?"* he remembered saying to her. *"It's what you came for, isn't it—to put it back?"* She had faced him with that fixed awful smile. *"Yes, of course,"* she had said. *"I must do that."*

What had she done then? She had turned her back, pulled open the drawer of the cherrywood table and then firmly closed it again. She had *pretended* to put the gun back in the drawer. Instead, she had slipped it into her handbag. Why? Nick searched his brain but came up with no answer.

His first impulse was to turn the whole matter over to Bacchus. This was his gun and his baby. But Bacchus, after giving his statement to the police, had abruptly paid his hotel bill and left for New York. There was nothing but to do as Letty asked.

After rejecting both the closet and the space under the bed,

Nick found an extra blanket folded away in a bureau drawer. He thrust the handbag under the blanket. Leaving the room, he took the precaution of hanging the Do Not Disturb sign on the knob outside. Hopefully, until he returned, his secret was safe.

All this had taken time. Rounding the hall, he saw Letty, very pale but dressed and waiting at the elevator. Lechay was on one side of her, a bellman with her luggage on the other.

They left the hotel by way of the basement. This was to avoid the detective in the lobby. Lechay also wanted to steer clear of inquisitive reporters who might be hanging about.

Lechay was already thinking of that morning's rehearsal, a crucial rehearsal beset with difficulties and without the star of the play. He left for the theater as soon as they were outside.

Nick kept a wary eye out all the way to the hospital but saw no sign of anyone following them. He paused at a stoplight long enough to hand Letty the wallet and checkbook. Her eyes flashed a frightened question at him, and he answered as quickly. "It's in my room. No one has seen it."

"You won't have to keep it long, Nick," she promised. "I didn't dare take it to the hospital. But I'll be out in a day or two. I'll—I'll think of something."

He asked why she had not put it back in the drawer where it belonged.

She was silent a long time, and then said, in a toneless voice, "I never should have taken it at all." She looked haggard and ill, and he did not want to press her as he had the night before. He let the subject drop.

He stayed beside her all the time she was being signed in and was still at her side when she was taken up to her room. There was too much they could not speak about, and they hardly talked at all. Yet he knew she wanted him there. He did not leave her until she was wheeled away through the doors of the X-ray room.

He spent the rest of the morning buying a small plastic suitcase with a particularly businesslike lock. He also bought two shirts, a plain black knit tie, a change of underwear and some small items he would need for a stay of two or three days. After this he went back to the hotel. He had thought of nothing all morning but the gun in his room.

As soon as he got there he stripped off his shirt and, wrapping it around his hand, extracted the gun from the handbag and placed it, together with the shirt, in the suitcase. This receptacle he locked and, after some thought, hid from sight on the top shelf of a closet. Pushed against the rear wall, it could not be seen from any point in the room. It was a dangerous hiding place, but until he found a better one it would have to do.

Half an hour later, showered, shaved and wearing one of his new shirts, he went down into the lobby where he bought the New York papers and picked up a copy of the *New Haven Register*. He read a review of *The Masquers* over scrambled eggs and coffee in a waffle shop down the street.

On Sunday the *Register* and *Courier Journal* came out under one masthead. Thus, there was only one New Haven review, but it was a review taken seriously in the profession.

The *Register* treated Letty with a good deal of kindness, but the honors of the evening were with Lilo, and the critic did not conceal it. Three full paragraphs were devoted to a performance described as "shattering, almost painful in its intensity." By comparison, Letty was hardly mentioned. A reference to "first-night nerves," put in to excuse her, only made it clear that the star had not come up even to an ordinary professional standard.

But if Letty was slighted in the notice, she was given ample space in the news and gossip columns. The New York papers carried the shooting of Ralph Jackman. The arrest of Letty's son, coupled with reports that she had collapsed in full view of a first-night audience, made very good copy indeed.

Nick visited the hospital again late that afternoon. This time he made it his business to look about rather carefully, but he saw no one in the corridor or waiting room who looked like a detective. Either the police had believed Lilo's story, or they were sure they had their man in Keith. Whatever the reason, they had apparently called off the watch on Letty.

The visit was brief. Letty looked exhausted, and except for

128

some irritable complaints about the tests she was undergoing, she had little to say.

Nick dined that evening with Ed Lamper and some of the actors in the hotel dining room. It was hardly a pleasant meal. The whole room was buzzing about the Jackman shooting, and at one point a woman with a loud voice exclaimed, "Oh, *she's* the one who did it. Everyone knows the son is just taking the rap!"

The actors carried it off with a cool irony, but they were the center of a hard curiosity and they resented it. There was an unspoken resentment against Letty too. Nick had an idea they would have openly criticized her if he had not been present. The whole cast thought she was mixed up somewhere in the Jackman affair and felt her illness was too conveniently timed. Members of the company had been questioned at length by the police that morning. They told themselves they had been treated like criminals, while the star had coolly taken herself out of reach.

Nick picked up the day's developments as the meal proceeded. Clarissa Howe was going on for Letty that night. A character actress named Anna Harkos was being rushed out to take over her role later in the week. But nobody believed the play would last that long. "Business is down already," Collier pointed out, "and she hasn't been out one day!"

There were some guarded references to Lilo, who had marched down to headquarters that morning and told the story that gave Letty her alibi. "She's a tough tootsie!" one of the actors murmured. "You've got to hand it to her!"

"Her career!" Collier remarked with a knowing shrug.

"She took a very big chance," someone murmured.

"And she might have spared herself the trouble," Sarah Hall put in quietly. "With Letty sick, we'll close anyway."

Only Ed Lamper still had hopes the play would survive. The playwright was in truly pitiable condition. His script had knocked around for years before it was sold. From the first day the whole production had teetered on the brink of disaster. Now, with the goal almost in sight, it was agony to face defeat.

"If only we could get to New York!" he said to Nick in a despairing undertone. "Joe Lechay believes in this play! He thinks we could make a go of it even without a star. This Anna Harkos is a damn good actress. And Lilo is tremendous. Everyone says so!"

The actors were sorry for Lamper, but they did not share his hopes. They were in a sorry situation, people losing their jobs, losing their livelihood. Still they managed to joke, to make light of their predicament. They were actors, after all; it was their tradition to take the bad with the good. When they trouped out to give their performance, Nick was sorry to see them go.

He spent a half hour leafing through a magazine in the lobby and then, restless, walked over to the university campus. He spent some time there, wandering around the Quadrangle and looking up at the room where he had slept that first year after the war. The world itself had changed so much he could hardly find his way back, even in memory. All he could recapture was a youthful certainty that everything was going to go on and on for a long time. Somehow, things stopped feeling that way as you got older.

He walked back slowly, thinking first about his youth and Petra, then about Letty sleeping now in her room at Grace New Haven. She had never been straight with him; he could not forgive her for that. She had used him without conscience. She had yet to prove she was not guilty as hell. At moments Nick felt even her illness might be some sort of dodge. Like the actors, he felt she had somehow faked it—*worked* it.

This darkest mood did not last long. The truth was, he simply did not believe her guilty. He was angry with her. That was the long and the short of it. Angry that she was implicated, that she had made such a mess of his life and her own. And having swung back to the beginning, he gave up, exhausted by the treadmill of his thoughts.

It was still depressingly early when he got back to the hotel. He wondered how he was to get through the rest of the evening—wondered how many such evenings there would be.

* * *

130

Monday began badly. Keith's arraignment was scheduled for nine in the morning, but hour after hour went by with no word from Harold Lasher. When Lasher finally called, it was late afternoon and Letty was in a terrible state. But the news was good. The arraigning judge had granted bail. Keith was out.

Whether it was relief about Keith, or because her illness had reached its peak, Letty began to improve. Her fever went down, she looked more herself again and she took her supper that evening sitting up in a chair.

Before he left that evening, Nick had a short talk with Dr. Christianson. This large-boned, laconic and formidably competent physician was apparently pleased with Letty's progress. The lab tests had shown nothing too alarming. A little elevation of the white count. A slight haziness in the lung X ray . . . nothing more specific than that. If she continued to do as well, he gave her a good chance of being up and around in time for the New York opening.

Letty received a great many flowers in the next days; the room was quite crowded with them. Everyone called; everyone sent wires and messages. And a whole group of the actors managed a visit one afternoon, bringing good news with them. The play was doing better than expected, with advance sales good to the end of the run. It looked as though they would survive and open in New York as scheduled. "All we need now is for you to get well," they told Letty, rallying her.

Now the play was doing better, the actors were sorry for their suspicions of Letty, who seemed to be really ill after all. They stood around her bed, giving her the gossip, the news. Lilo and Harkos had already had a cat-and-dog fight; they no longer talked when they met. Harkos was a strong performer, but not a patch on Letty. And lastly, Letty had to get well, because the whole thing was no fun without her!

She laughed at all the stories, at times with rather wet lashes. She was pleased her friends had come, pleased she had not been forgotten. But the long visit tired her. Her fever went up again that night, and new tests had to be ordered.

"There is a definite pneumonic process," Dr. Christianson

explained to Nick. "It's quite clear on the last X rays. There's no need to panic. We have new techniques these days. The antibiotics have helped—still, pneumonia is nothing to fool with. She's got to realize that."

It seemed the New York premiere was out.

Letty seemed almost to have expected the blow, along with her other disappointments. Though she had tried not to show it, the New Haven review had hurt her terribly. She had waited day after day for some word from Keith; though she did not expect him to come, she had hoped he might perhaps call, speak to her. It was many days before she understood he would not even do that. And although she did not complain, seemed, indeed, to understand it, she grew each day a little more silent, a little more inside herself.

On the morning after his talk with Dr. Christianson, Nick answered an early knock and found Leo Arnaboldi at his door. The little actor gazed at him warily, none too sure of his welcome. He had kept out of Nick's way ever since their words backstage. He hid his embarrassment now under a rather stiff air of dignity. He had brought with him a newspaper folded back to an inside page. Nick's eye was immediately drawn to a rough pen-and-ink reproduction of an already familiar symbol. K'an had made its way into the columns of a major New York newspaper! Arnaboldi had marked off the accompanying item with a pencil.

Nick, thoroughly disturbed, read through the article again. He looked up to find Arnaboldi anxiously watching him. "What do you think?" Arnaboldi stammered out. "It's silly nonsense, isn't it? Magic books? Hocus-pocus? Is anyone going to take all that seriously?"

Nick did not know how to answer. It seemed to him disastrous that the threatening hexagram had come to light at all.

"But it's just a silly scrawl!" Arnaboldi persisted. "How can it possibly mean anything?"

"If Keith sent Jackman a threat—*any* kind of threat—it brings in the possibility of premeditation."

BIZARRE CLUE IN JACKMAN CASE
LINKS MYSTIC BOOK TO FATALITIES

Police today disclosed that a blood-stained note inscribed with a curious symbol found in the pocket of the late Dr. Ralph Jackman has been traced to an ancient Chinese book known as the I Ching, or *Book of Changes*. When decoded, the cryptograph was found to represent a prophecy of impending doom. Police have reason to believe that playwright Kenneth Stramm received the same prediction from the occult book just before the freak fall that led to his death in September. They are speculating on a possible link between the two cases.

Death Threat a "Joke"?

Keith Tilden, now out on bail and awaiting trial in the Jackman shooting, told reporters the threatening hexagram could only have been sent as "some kind of joke." The son of actress Lorette Harris, Mr. Tilden admits familiarity with the I Ching, a book enjoying wide popularity among activist students who believe the mystic volume foretells the future.

Reproduction of the I Ching cryptograph found on the body of Dr. Ralph Jackman.

"Premeditation. That's bad." Arnaboldi gnawed at his lower lip. "I know premeditation is bad."

"Let's hope it won't come to that." Nick scanned the lines again, muttering aloud, "'Playwright Stramm—same prophecy—freak fall—'" He looked up, frowning. "How the devil did the police find out you were fooling with the I Ching that night?"

"Jackman probably told them," Arnaboldi replied mournfully. "Poor Ralph! He kept giving them a bit here—a bit there. He thought they'd be satisfied and leave him alone. It only made them go after him more."

"Maybe Harold Lasher can fix this," Nick said slowly. "I don't see what anyone else can do." He handed back the paper, but

Arnaboldi lingered. He was nerving himself to say something more.

"They're not going to rake up that other thing, are they? The business about Stramm?" A faint line of sweat glistened on his forehead.

"I don't know anything about that," Nick said coldly. How terrified they all were, he thought, at any mention of the Stramm affair!

In the end, Arnaboldi crept out humbly with his paper. Nick felt rather sorry for him. He had probably come in the hopes that Nick would be friendly again.

When he got to the hospital he found Letty deep in a long-distance conversation with Harold Lasher. The newspaper, opened at the story, was spread out on her bed. When she hung up, she remained a moment with closed eyes and then asked Nick if he had seen the article.

"Yes, I've seen it."

"This is bad," Letty said.

Nick said nothing.

"Keith has got to jump bail," Letty said. "I can't make Lasher understand. He hasn't got a chance after this! They'll send him up if he goes on trial. They'll send him up for life!"

Nick could find nothing to say. He thought Letty was right.

The Flame

Its coming is sudden.
It flames up—
dies down—
is thrown away—

Midge arrived on Thursday of the following week. She swept in on all of them in a high gale of efficiency, and within an hour dismissed a nurse, engaged another, conferred with Letty's doctors and began complicated arrangements to ship some of Letty's belongings to New York and transfer others to her own room at the hotel.

For five hours, while her husband lay dying, Midge had stuck to her story at police headquarters. She had found Ralph Jackman at the foot of the staircase. She had seen no gun. She knew of no one with a grudge against him. Five hours of questioning had not stirred her from this position, and in the end they let her go. Two days later she had gone through the additional ordeal of burying her husband under particularly grueling circumstances.

Midge had cared more for little Ralph Jackman than most people knew, and all this had left its mark. Her eyes had a tendency to fill at the slightest emotion, and the face she brought to New Haven was still blank and white with shock.

Nevertheless, she was there. The shocked face had been subjected to a cosmetic mask, and she arrived correct at every point with proper furs and floating veils. Any anger she had ever felt with Letty for stealing the gun had vanished in a wave of concern about her illness.

A few of the actors were on hand to murmur their sympathy. Midge cried some of those easy new tears, and told everyone Letty would not be in this condition if Ralph Jackman were alive. When Arnaboldi ventured to remark that Letty was in excellent hands, Midge turned on him in violent contradiction. "She's not responding!" she snapped. "I've talked to her doctors. There's a resistance to the antibiotic!"

She finally swept back to Letty's room, leaving the others exchanging expressive looks. "Poor dear Midge!" Sarah Hall murmured. "Has she really persuaded herself that funny little man was a great doctor?"

Clayton Collier cleared his throat. "I don't like to speak ill of the dead, but he was not the greatest medical light of the century. It's no wonder Letty isn't responding! He shot her full of penicillin every time the wind changed!"

There was a general feeling that it was a bit hard to put up with Midge. Still the actors were glad she was there—someone who would really look after things.

For Nick, her arrival meant release. He had stayed on for many reasons, but mainly he had stayed because Letty had no one else. Someone had to be there with her, someone had to speak to her doctors, see that she paid her bills, fend off the reporters who prowled around the corridors. Now Midge would take over. Truth to tell, Nick was impatient to be off. He needed to sort out his feelings, needed to get some distance from all that had happened. Above all, there was the gun. He had lost too much time already, and he made plans to leave the following day.

"You must be good, and get well soon," he said to Letty next morning.

"I'll be all right," she answered nervously. "Everyone takes care of me."

"It's just a matter of days now!" Midge put in. "They'd let her go now. They just want to be doubly sure."

"Yes! Yes!" Letty broke in again impatiently. "Nick knows all that."

She had just come back from the X-ray room. She wanted to sit up a little longer and the wheelchair was moved closer to the window where she could get the sun on her face. A light blanket lay over her knees. She had lost weight in the hospital, and her features stood out today with an unusual sharp clarity. She had dressed for Nick's last visit in a rose-colored robe of cut velvet. She was even wearing her emerald ring.

"The play opens this Wednesday," she remarked, toying nervously with the lace at her throat. "I'm sorry to let the actors down."

Nick said the main thing now was to get well.

Midge declared Letty would surprise everyone. "You'll see. We'll have her at that opening yet."

"There's no hope of that," Letty said. She was silent and added, "It doesn't matter, of course. The play will be a success whether I'm there or not."

Midge said with scorn, "Not without you, it won't be!"

"The play will be a success with me or without me," Letty said.

For a moment nobody spoke.

"There's something I want you to do for me," she resumed, speaking to Nick. "It's a message. For Keith. Will you give it to him?"

"Of course."

She turned a little in the chair. "I want Midge to hear it too."

"I'm listening, dear." Midge was moving about the room, arranging things. "But you know, you'll be seeing Keith yourself in a few days."

"I'm not sure I'll be seeing much of Keith after this," Letty said slowly.

"Well, go on, dear. We're listening!" She signaled silently across the room, telling Nick not to argue.

After thinking a little, Letty said, "I don't believe you know it, Nick, but Keith has always looked up to you. He thinks you're a great man, a great artist. He doesn't have that kind of respect for most of the people around me. That's why I want you to be the one who—who gives him the message."

Nick waited.

"Keith was there, you see." Letty was thinking it out as she spoke. "He was in the house when it happened."

"You mean when Stramm—" Nick's attention suddenly sharpened.

"No! No!" She swept that idea away. "Keith was *in the house! When his father died!*"

So it was John Keith Tilden who haunted her.

"We said terrible things to each other that day, John and I," Letty said. Her face had gone haggard. "We forgot about Keith. Forgot he might be listening—a boy of fourteen. I never knew how much of it he heard. But he changed after that. He was never the same again."

Nick said, "What is it you want me to tell him?"

She said slowly, "You must tell Keith I did not kill his father—that I had no guilt in his father's death." He tried to speak, but she held up her hand and said sharply, "Wait! There's something more!"

She paused a very long time and something cold seemed to go over Nick. The room was so still they could hear children playing somewhere. At last she went on, slowly and clearly. "You must tell Keith it was I who killed Kenneth Stramm. I did it alone. Nobody but myself had any part in it. That's—my message."

138

Letty's arms had fallen limp at her sides. "Midge is here," she said in a low voice. "She knows I have told the truth."

Not by a movement or the flicker of an eye did Nick reveal the terrible shock he had just received.

Midge stood motionless, her face a white blur in the shadow near the door.

After drawing several deep breaths, Letty lifted her head and spoke in her ordinary voice. "And now you must go and get your train, Nick. I'm tired, and I want to rest."

She rose. The blanket slipped to the floor. Midge helped her across the room. She moved slowly, as though she had all at once grown older. But she turned again and said with a smile, "We had it all, Nick. Love was real. It was there for us. We just weren't up to it—that's all."

"We'll talk about it some other time," he said.

"No we won't!" she shook her head at him quaintly. "There's nothing to talk about. Not anymore. We lost it, Nick. And we'll never get it back!"

This time he remained silent. She sighed as Midge helped her into her bed. But when he rose to go she spoke again, her voice up at a strong, normal volume. "Nick?"

"Yes?"

"Keith has to be told to jump bail. He doesn't stand a chance if the case goes to trial. Tell Harold I said so."

"I'll tell him."

"And you'll give Keith my message?"

"Yes, Letty. I'll give him your message."

"That's all right then." And turning comfortably on her side, "I want to sleep now. I'm tired."

As soon as they were out in the corridor Midge burst into tears. "Letty never harmed anyone in her life!" she declared passionately. "She tried to *save* that awful man!"

Nick gave a rather dazed laugh. "Did she really want me to tell Keith she—"

"Of course not!" Midge denied it fiercely. "She's wandering— feverish! Couldn't you see she wasn't in her right mind?" But her desperate denials died into a silence under his gaze.

139

For a moment he simply searched the face under that hard, flawless maquillage, searched it narrowly and curiously. The elaborate pretense they had both erected fell away at that instant. There was only that close, cold scrutiny.

"Well, good-bye," Nick said at last in a colorless voice. "I've got to go back and get my train."

"Nick!" Midge called. She looked frightened and alone standing there in the corridor. "You'll be seeing us, won't you? You'll be seeing us in New York?"

"I don't know." He considered it, his head a little to one side. "I pretty much got my walking papers in there, wouldn't you say?"

"Don't leave her!" Midge pleaded. She moved a step closer. "Trust her!" she begged.

He took the hand she stretched out toward him, patted it once or twice. "I don't trust any of you, Midge!" he said. "But you're a good kid just the same. Take care of things!"

He drove back over the bridge to the hotel and went to his room. The enormity of what he had just heard was breaking over him in a succession of shocks. Feverish? Wandering in her mind? Nick did not think so. She had openly confessed to the murder of Stramm.

The whole ugly swarm of his suspicions had come alive again. Bacchus, Arnaboldi, the girl—they were all in on it. They were all hypocrites and liars, but the woman was the worst; she had taken him in with the shop-soiled wares of the whore. When he thought of the past weeks he was appalled at his folly. He had protected her at his own deadly risk. He had driven her to New Haven fresh from Jackman's corpse. He had lived all those days with the murder gun in his room. She had made him an accessory, if not an actual accomplice, to her crimes. And now that his usefulness had ended she had pushed him out? With a glib phrase or two about *love?* "We weren't up to it." What could she mean by that except that *he* was the one who had failed.

"Easy enough to talk about love," he answered her now in his mind. "Easy to talk about trust while you were walking around gunning down everyone who threatened your interests. Or getting your son to do it for you!" He thought of the message he was to give Keith, and fury gripped him. Let her deliver her own murderous messages to her son. He was through with both of them!

The gun, still wrapped in his shirt, lay at the bottom of the suitcase. The sight of it sickened him anew. This was the weapon that had killed Jackman. The police were looking for it even now. Fool, to have kept it. Fool, deserving any punishment he got!

A mix of voices in the hall froze him. He stood with lowered head, immobile and listening. Two people coming out of the elevator. Clayton Collier and Lilo. A casual word. A short laugh. They parted. Someone was coming toward him down the hall. On a sudden impulse, Nick threw open his door.

She stopped dead as she saw him. She was wearing a storm coat with a red fox collar, and her blond hair had been tossed about by the wind. For a moment she was motionless, her eyes on his, then she continued on her way, moving sinuously in her high-heeled boots. Nick heard her key turning as she opened her door, but though he listened there was no sound of the door closing again.

This curious encounter was not their first. She had a way of passing him in the hall, of appearing beside him at the newsstand in the lobby or at the counter in the coffee shop where he took his breakfast. She was always alone. She did not seem to care that nobody in the company liked or trusted her. There was something almost criminal about her. She had the dangerous strength of those who have hit bottom and have nothing more to fear.

Nick admired strength of any kind, but he could not help despising her greed. She had taken the play away from Letty. Wasn't that enough for her? Did she have to have the sculptor friend too?

Since he did not care to give her that victory, Nick had never broken his silence, never given her more than a cold nod. But it was all smashed up now, and he didn't care about anything. If the girl still wanted her victory he saw no reason not to let her

141

have it. Her room was diagonally across from where Letty's had been. When he came around the hall, she was standing in the open door. She had not taken off the storm coat, had not even moved, so tensely had she waited.

He reached out and touched the red fox collar. Her eyes blazed out at him. "Shut the door!" she said.

There was a fast train to New York at 1:12. But there were other trains after that, and it made so little difference. He walked in and let the door shut behind him. "You should take off your coat," he said in a thick voice. "Here. Let me help you."

There was some tricky way the coat fastened. It took a little time, but he found it.

It was midafternoon when he got back to his room. He had finished packing and was leaving for the station when the call came that sent him hurrying back to the hospital.

Midge was waiting for him in the corridor. "It was a sudden bad spell," Midge said. "She got a chill; she couldn't seem to breathe—"

"But I was just here!" Nick interrupted harshly. "I was here today. She was getting better!"

"It was after you left. There was a chill. She couldn't get her breath—"

Nick didn't want to hear any more. He began striding down the corridor. Midge caught up with him at Letty's door. "There's no use going in," she told him breathlessly. "They've taken her away. To the intensive care unit."

He went in nevertheless. It was a big empty sunny room. He wondered what they had done with the flowers. She had always had such masses of them.

Later that day he and Midge had a little visit with Dr. Christianson in the waiting room. The doctor sat with them quite a long time, talking to them like an old friend in a low, confidential voice. The infection hadn't looked that bad on the first lab tests. On the whole she seemed to be doing fairly well. But the pneumonia had shown up clearly on the second slides.

142

Apparently some strain of the organism that resisted the penicillin. She had improved for a day or so on a different antibiotic. But a few hours ago a sudden downward turn. Uncontrollable chills, signs of septicemia— The low grave voice went on and on . . . negative factors . . . run down physically . . . severe psychological pressure . . . always hope, of course. . . .

Midge continually interrupted with questions she wanted answered. Septicemia . . . overwhelming infection—to Midge these words meant only that Something had to be Done. She was gearing up for battle. Nick felt only a blankness—as though the rules had been switched on him in the middle of the game. Stramm and Jackman, after all, had made a kind of frightful sense. Clearly, it had served someone's purposes that they should die. But no human hand had struck Letty down. This was simply Death, caring nothing for anyone's purposes. And Death changed everything. Death changed the lenses inside your eyes and made you see another picture. No matter how right you may have been, Death put you in the wrong.

Bacchus came up by train the following day. He stayed a long time in the dim room where Letty lay, and his face was a mask when he came out. He spoke only to Lechay and after that left immediately for the station and New York. Nick got no more than a brief glimpse of him as he walked past the waiting room.

On Sunday, Harold Lasher came up and brought Keith Tilden with him. But by that time it was doubtful if Letty could recognize Keith or anyone else.

Such crowds of visitors came that Sunday that they overflowed out into the corridor. The New Haven actors were there in force. It was their last visit; they were leaving the following day for New York, where the play was to open. Quite a number of other theatrical lights showed up too. Everyone was shocked by Letty's illness, but with so many friends unexpectedly meeting, some quiet shop talk was unavoidable. There were moments, in fact, when the waiting room seemed more a club than a hospital.

143

Nick was glad to see everyone, grateful for the company. He was privately dreading the moment when the actors would go, leaving him alone with Midge.

But it wasn't bad, he found, when everyone had left New Haven. He did not often go into the dimly lit room where Letty battled with her all-powerful foe, nor did he ever stay there long. He spent his days in the waiting room, a more pleasant and spacious place. There were magazines. Though nobody ever turned it on, there was a television set. Visitors came and sat occasionally. Patients wandered in from time to time in their hospital robes. Nick became quite attached to an old Scotsman, himself a doctor, who told him the whole story of his life one long afternoon.

No, it wasn't bad when the others had gone. He and Midge drew closer. They took most of their meals together now. One night they even went to the movies together.

Midge was putting great hopes in the new antibiotic. She used so many medical terms these days she might have been a doctor herself. The names of great specialists were always on her lips. She talked a good deal about transferring Letty to another hospital—Johns Hopkins or Harkness Pavilion. Nick never contradicted, never argued with her, but he didn't really listen. He knew Letty was going to die. He had known it as soon as he got the telephone call. After all that had happened, what in the world could the woman do *but* die?

And so he was not really surprised some days later, when at six in the evening—with lights going on all over New Haven—Letty did, very quietly, die.

Breakthrough

Owing to circumstances,
there is a change in conditions,
a breakthrough.
The strong determine
the affairs of the weak.

"I don't understand!" Bacchus declared. "Are you saying this thing has been in your possession all this time?"

Nick shrugged. "Ever since she gave it to me."

"And you've kept it until now? Simply kept it?"

"What else could I do?"

"My dear man, in your place I would not have kept it for a day! I have no idea what you can do about it now. Hand it over to the police. Throw it in a sewer. Stow it away in one of those lockers in Grand Central Station. Isn't that what people in books are always doing with such things?"

On arriving at Washington Street, Nick had immediately gone up to the parlor floor, taking with him the plastic suitcase he had bought in New Haven. He'd found Bacchus at the great mahogany desk in the room that served as both study and bar. He was consulting a volume of rare prints, checking the illustrations in the book against a group of quick wash drawings of his own. At the moment, however, he was examining neither prints nor sketches. A cigarette holder between his teeth, he was squinting with disfavor at the gaping suitcase Nick had placed on his desk and the unpleasant object he had drawn out of it.

"So you think I should get rid of it?" Nick asked, pursuing the question.

"You are certainly in a bad position holding on to it," Bacchus pointed out. "The decision, of course, rests with you."

"I suppose it does. But tell me, Bacchus—do you yourself feel no responsibility at all?"

"My dear Nick!" Bacchus stared at him, astonished. "Why in the world should I?"

Nick said gently, "After all, Bill, it's your gun."

Bacchus carefully closed the volume of prints, lifted himself with an effort from his chair and said, "Come with me, Nick. I want to show you something."

He led the way up the stairs to the second floor and threw open the door to the master bedroom. The plum velvet drapes were drawn back now, and the whole beautifully ordered room gleamed and glowed in the afternoon sunlight.

Bacchus walked into the center of the floor. "Now! You say Letty was standing just about here? By the bed?"

"With the gun in her hand. She was trying to hide it, of course, but she couldn't be too obvious, so she didn't succeed very well. I told her to put the gun back. She turned and opened the drawer of the table there. But for some reason she put the gun into her handbag, not into the drawer."

"I think I can explain why she did that," Bacchus said. "You see, Nick, there was just no room for it in here!" And sliding the drawer out to its fullest length he revealed to Nick what Letty had undoubtedly seen before him: a gun was already lying there.

"*This* is my gun," Bacchus announced calmly. "I do not and have not at any time possessed any other."

Nick was making an effort to readjust his ideas. "Then the gun I just showed you—"

"The gun you just showed me is a Colt .38. This is a Smith and Wesson. Same caliber, but entirely different make."

"So there were two guns in this affair!"

"Jackman was definitely not shot with mine. That was proved by an official ballistics test."

"They put your gun through ballistics?"

"There was no way I could prevent it, since it was registered in my name. I was told in New Haven I could either give it up or they would get a warrant for search and seizure and do the job without my permission. That was why I left so suddenly for New York. I preferred to be present when these men entered my home." A baleful gleam came into his eye. "I also wanted to clear up the mess you made when you rode roughshod over these premises playing Arsène Lupin!" He shut the drawer smartly. "Well, they put it through their test. When they returned it, they told me it was out of the picture in the Jackman shooting. I was relieved to hear it. I was also surprised. Keith still has the key to this house. I was certain he must have entered during my absence, gotten my gun and shot the doctor with it."

"Apparently that's what Letty thought too. As a matter of fact, so did I."

"Well, we were wrong. All three of us."

"Keith got his gun somewhere else then," Nick said thoughtfully.

"They're easy enough to get," Bacchus remarked. "Anyone who knows the ropes can still go upstate and get himself a gun."

"Y-yes." Something had clicked in Nick's brain. It was a casual word someone had dropped not long ago, a remark of no importance. He blew air out slowly. "This puts rather a different face on things. And I'm damned if I know what to do about it."

"Well," said Bacchus, "you'd better do something soon."

"This is a big case, Nick!" Harold Lasher said. "A lot of publicity. A lot of glamorous names. There's a full-size search on for that gun. Why did you wait so long? Why didn't you bring it to me sooner?"

"Well, I've brought it to you now," Nick answered with some grimness.

"But ten days have gone by!" Lasher was laughing helplessly at the dangerous ignorance of it. "Don't you realize the spot you've got me into, the spot you've gotten *yourself* into?"

"I know it looks bad. I shouldn't have held on to it."

"Man, you've concealed evidence! You've concealed crucial evidence in a case involving a homicide!"

Nick heaved a sigh and pressed his forehead with two fingers. "I don't know if I can make you understand this, Harold. I thought Letty might have killed Jackman. Even after Keith was arrested, I still thought she might be implicated. She could have been there when Keith shot him. It even went through my mind that she could have put Keith up to it!"

"Really?" Lasher was intrigued by such a mental process. "You really thought Letty would ask Keith to—?"

"I caught her with a gun in her hand. Jackman had just been shot. I don't know what the hell I believed. I'm still not sure."

"Hm. Interesting. Suspecting the worst, you remained so involved as to keep the gun, and all that time? I can see you really were in a predicament. Humanly speaking, of course." Lasher corrected himself. "Legally you had no right to hold on to that gun. No right at all."

Nick sighed. "She asked me to keep it until she came out of the hospital. I thought she had a right to make her own decisions about it. She was on the phone with you every day. She could have told you about the gun. I didn't feel I had a right to do it if she didn't."

"I can see that," Lasher acknowledged, "but weren't you *curious*? Didn't you even *question* her?"

"I questioned her," Nick said with a mirthless laugh. He spoke again, soberly. "I deviled that girl very badly out there, Harold. I kept hammering at her for the truth, the truth—and what she needed was a little human kindness. I was trying to help her, but she'd been through too much. I should have realized she was cracking up—"

148

Lasher reached out and touched his shoulder. "Come on, guy!" His voice was rough, comradely. "You were with her right to the end. Everyone says you were fantastic. Absolutely devoted."

"I did a few things for her," Nick acknowledged quietly. "I just did them all too late."

"Well, no use dwelling on the past." Lasher was studying the gun. "I've got to hand this thing over, and I've got to do it so neither of us gets hurt." He scratched his ear. "It was bad when it disappeared, but I'm not sure this isn't worse. If they trace it to some group of wild-eyed young bomb-throwers the jury is going to throw the book at us!"

"Where does Keith say he got it?"

"Keith told it six different ways," Lasher said gloomily. "When they picked him up, he swore he wasn't anywhere near Jackman all that day. That was Version A. After the doorman identified him, he came up with Version B. He did go to see Jackman, but for reducing pills. They tripped him on that one with no trouble at all. He had no pills and no prescription that would support his story. That was when he came up with Version C. The version he gave me. According to Version C, it was Jackman who had the gun. Keith swears he never saw it before."

"Did you believe it?"

"It doesn't matter what I believe or don't believe," Lasher said wearily. "It's what the jury thinks that counts. Suppose you were sitting on the case. The kid sends Jackman a threat. They meet, and Jackman pulls out a gun and threatens him. When Jackman's gun goes off, who does it kill? Jackman. The kid runs out, leaving the gun on a staircase, but strangely enough, the gun is never seen again. It's disappeared. How would that sound to you?"

"Pretty thin. All the same, we have some facts now that we didn't have before. Keith did leave the gun on the staircase just as he claims."

"Yes. Now you tell me!" Lasher shook his head reproachfully. "Crazy thing for Letty to do, running off with the gun like that. Typical, of course. She thought she was helping Keith." He sighed. "I don't see this gets us very far. I suppose we could bring Letty into it, but it wouldn't help Keith much."

Nick did not speak for a time. Then he said quietly, "There's something I want to tell you, Harold. It's about Jackman. When he came to see me that day he was a badly frightened man. But in a queer kind of way he was also a proud man. Something important had happened to him. It was like a new role he had been given in life. He kept throwing funny little hints at me. For instance, he made a point of telling me he had driven up to Monticello that day. He and Midge have a small summer place up there. I thought at the time he must have gone to see a patient. Now I believe he was hinting at something more dramatic."

"What's that?"

"I think Jackman went to Monticello in order to buy himself a gun. And I think that's what he did do."

Lasher thought it over. "Do you have any reason to think so? Besides a casual mention of the place?"

"Well, he was carrying a small attaché case with him. Not the sort of thing a doctor usually carries. He was worried about it, didn't want to put it down. He also told me, very pointedly, that he was 'taking steps to protect himself.' I assumed he meant he was appealing to the police for protection. Now I think he was telling me he had bought a gun."

"It's an attractive theory," Lasher said a little dubiously. "I don't know if it would hold up."

"Can you do anything with it at all?"

"I don't know. We'd have to have proof—witnesses." He thought a moment. "Still, we've got nothing else. It might be worth a try." He weighed it another moment or two. "Hell with 'em," he said, making up his mind. "They've looked ten days. Let them look a little longer."

"What are you going to do?"

"I don't know yet. Leave this thing here, and let me think about it. I'll talk to a few people, see if your idea checks out anywhere."

Nick got up. "Will you let me know?"

150

"I will if anything develops. It's a long shot, Nick, remember that."

Lasher walked him to the door and they stood silent a moment. They were both thinking of the same thing. "It's at two this afternoon," Nick finally said. "You'll be there, I suppose."

"Oh, yes," Lasher said with a sigh. "She was one of my oldest friends. I loved Letty. I'll be there."

It was a big turnout and quite impressive. Several thousand massed on the street outside the chapel, and police lined up to see that order was maintained. People had come, of course, just to watch the celebrities drive up in their cars. The freaks and loonies were all out too—one had to expect that. A few voices shouted "Murderer!" when Keith Tilden walked through the police lines, and there was another faint jeer when Bacchus walked through. But Letty's death had brought about a popular reaction in her favor. Most of the crowd was there because they were sorry she was gone. There was a surprising number of older people, quietly dressed men and women who remembered her before Hollywood, remembered the days when she had starred on Broadway.

Inside, the rooms were crowded and very warm. A big part of the theatrical world was on hand for the occasion. A good many people he did not know made it a point to come up and say a few words to Nick, and he realized after a while that he was regarded here as the chief mourner. The New Haven actors fluttered around him, full of sympathy. Midge embraced him with a face contorted by grief and told him once again that Letty would not have died if only Ralph Jackman had been there to save her.

Nick excused himself. He had just caught sight of Keith and Bettina talking to Harold Lasher. Bettina looked pale and shabby, and she had a haunted look in her eyes. Keith had changed too. He had grown thin, almost gaunt. He had also shaved off his beard and was unexpectedly handsome without it. Nick was startled to see how much he resembled his mother.

Nick wanted a word with Keith, but it was hard getting through the crowded room, and he retreated rather than come face to face with Lilo. She was chatting easily with Bacchus and Joe Lechay, rocking back and forth on her high heels, one hand on her hip, her fur jacket open; and Nick hated all her brutal young ambition.

Two people who have come together to do harm to a third are not fond of each other afterward. She was as willing as Nick to avoid the encounter.

The services in the main chapel were long, the hall badly lit and overheated. A number of theatrical bigwigs spoke, but nothing they said sounded remotely to Nick like Letty. He was glad when it was over and they were outside again, waiting for the limousines that would take them on their sad excursion.

He made the trip with a group of people who apparently owned a small factory upstate. They turned out to be relatives of Letty, but they could hardly have been close, for they chatted quietly and comfortably of their own affairs all the long way out.

A pale fleshy young man in a beret who sat up front with the driver turned from time to time and smiled encouragingly at Nick through the dividing glass. He looked familiar, and Nick placed him as possibly one of the actors he had met in New Haven.

It was not until after the business at the graveside that he got a chance to talk to Keith Tilden. The crowd of mourners were already walking away up the path, but Keith lingered, wanting a moment at the grave alone. Nick approached him there and told him he had a message from his mother. "She was ill at the time," he explained rather colorlessly. "She may have been wandering, feverish. But I promised her I would deliver it."

He did not know how Keith might react to this announcement, but the young man's answer was simply, "What did she say?" And he inclined his dark head so as to miss no part of it.

"She wanted me to tell you two things," Nick began with an effort. "The first was that your father died by his own hand and that she had no guilt in his death."

For a moment the dark eyes—Letty's eyes—flashed intimately

152

into his own. "I know who was guilty in my father's death," Keith said. He waited for the rest of it.

Nick braced himself and went on. "She asked me to tell you that it was she who killed Kenneth Stramm. She asked me to say that she did it alone—that no one else had any part in it."

Keith took it in with a quiet nod, his eyes somewhere on the horizon. "Yes," he said finally, "she wanted very much for me to think so."

That was all. Keith thanked him and walked away. Lasher and Bettina were waiting for him a short way up the path. He joined them, and a moment later Nick watched him follow Bettina into Lasher's Cadillac. Except for Lasher and that brief exchange with Nick at the graveside, hardly a soul that day had approached him or given him a word.

The young man in the beret joined Nick as he waited for his limousine. After a silence he remarked with a sigh that nobody had thought things would end this way.

"Very sad," Nick agreed.

The young man ruminated. "All the same, she said something remarkable. It was when she was very near the end. Do you remember? We took turns going into her room. It was only a day or two before we left for New York."

"Yes. I remember." Nick suddenly recognized the young man as Ed Lamper, the playwright.

"Well, I went in when it was my turn. I was told I should only stay a moment. She was in an oxygen tent and very weak, but I could see she wanted to tell me something. I leaned over as far as I could, and she whispered that the play was going to be a success, that I had nothing to fear."

"She told me the same thing," Nick mused. "She seemed very sure of it."

"Well, she repeated it to me several times. Her not being there would make no difference, she said. The play would be a tremendous success."

Nick smiled. "And is it?"

"Haven't you seen the reviews?" Lamper could not hide his

153

joy. "It's the biggest thing on Broadway! Standing room every night, tickets selling months ahead— People say there's never been anything like it with a dramatic show! They say we'll run for years if this keeps up."

"I'm glad, Ed," Nick said. "I'm glad for all of you." And in a way he really was.

The limusine pulled up, and they got in. The long trip to the city began. The strains of the day had tired the family group. Talk in the back of the limousine was desultory, disjointed.

The lines of some poem were going through Nick's head. An odd thing, hardly a poem at all.

> *When two people are one in their inmost hearts*
> *They shatter even the strength of iron or of bronze.*

The lines kept repeating themselves over and over in his mind. He had no idea where they were from or where he had heard them.

> *When two people are one in their inmost hearts*
> *They shatter even the strength of iron or of bronze.*

"Even the strength of iron or of bronze," Nick suddenly said, speaking aloud.

A surprised silence greeted the words, but the limousine sped on, and nobody asked what they meant.

Three days later the call from Harold Lasher came through. "Can you get over to the office today, Nick?"

"Sure I can. Do you have news?"

"The best!" Lasher sounded jubilant. "Come at six. We'll be able to talk."

The floor was already deserted when Nick got there, but a lady at the desk told Nick he was expected and buzzed Lasher on the intercom. In a minute or two the lawyer stuck his head into the hall, a little-boy grin on his face. "C'mon in, Armisen!" he called out exuberantly. The woman at the desk shook her head, smiling.

Lasher began as soon as they were alone. "This is it, Nick. We've hit pay dirt."

"Let's hear!" Nick sat down to listen.

"The whole thing went smooth as silk. You were right about Jackman. The man left a trail a mile wide. He *wanted* people to know what he had done. Dropped hints about it all over the place!"

"Tell me what happened!"

"It was easy! Jackman's receptionist was a Helen Landau— nice kid lives out in Brooklyn with her parents. I took her out to lunch and got her to talk. Turns out she'd been looking around for another job for some time. She had a feeling Jackman was cracking up."

"Did she know anything about a trip to Monticello?"

"Yes, she did. Jackman told her in the morning that he was driving up there. He got back late that afternoon and made a big point of telling her again. She was bored to death with his mysterious hints about Monticello. When she was leaving the office that night she found he'd managed to "accidentally" drop a sales slip on her desk—a slip from a Monticello store. She was out of patience with him and threw the slip into a drawer, thinking she'd give it to him on Monday. Well, by Monday, of course, Jackman was dead. She told the police he had talked about a trip to Monticello, but she was rattled and forgot about the sales slip."

"Did the police go up there?"

"I'm pretty sure they did. But chances are, they didn't find anyone that had seen Jackman that day. I doubt he spent much time visiting with neighbors."

"What about the sales slip?"

"The Landau girl came across it her last day when she was clearing out her desk. She was scared to death, thought she'd committed some kind of crime. But she's a good kid. She liked Keith. She knew I was fighting for him, and when I said it was important, she promised she'd dig the thing out and send it to me. Want to see it?" Lasher took an envelope from his desk, extracted a strip of paper from it, and passed it to Nick. It was an ordinary sales slip from a Monticello store called Leverett's. The slip was made out for a ninety-five-dollar purchase.

"Leverett's?"

"Sporting goods store. I went up yesterday with some photographs. One of them was a photo of Jackman. They've got two salesmen in the firearms department. The older one picked out Jackman's photo right away. Remembered him because he was so jumpy and nervous. The younger man had made the actual sale. He was pretty jumpy about it himself, but he'd done a fairly good job of covering. Jackman was a doctor, after all, with a bona-fide residence up there. There was probably some hanky-panky—maybe a hundred or so passed under the table. But the sale was listed in the regular way with a license number attached for the gun. The number was a phony, of course, but the salesman can always claim he took it in good faith."

"So it was Jackman who had the gun." Nick mused. "Keith's story was true after all."

"It was true," Lasher agreed, "but what good was it? We had nothing but his word. We've got a lot more now than that. We can produce Helen Landau. We can produce the salesman who sold him the gun. We've got a receipt for the gun! Our client acted in self-defense, and we've proved it. In fact, if the D.A. is smart—and I happen to know he is—there won't be a trial at all."

"Then it's all cleared up," Nick said thoughtfully.

"I think it will be."

"But we still don't know—" Nick stopped abruptly.

"Still don't know what, Nick?"

"About Kenneth Stramm."

Lasher looked at him curiously. "You have some ideas about that business, Nick?"

"None whatever."

"Then I'd say let it alone. Stramm and Jackman are gone, but

156

we're a lot closer to saving Keith Tilden." He clapped Nick on the shoulder in congratulation. "You've done a great thing, Nick. A marvelous thing. You've given the boy a chance!"

But Nick shook his head and said, "I didn't do it for Keith."

Gathering Together

Gathering together amid sighs.
There will be no error if we advance,
but we may suffer some regret.

High over the street the electric sign spelled it out: THE MASQUERS, and above it, in blazing lights, the name ANNA HARKOS. The play was well into its second smash season when Nick Armisen, passing through the Times Square area, saw the sign against the sky. Moved by an emotion he did not analyze, Nick retraced his steps and walked into the theater. A number of publicity stills were displayed in the lobby. He spent about ten minutes there, looking at these photographs rather closely.

Here were the actors again, just as he remembered them. Clayton Collier as the Showmaster. Arnaboldi in his Clown's costume. The giant Slave of Sam Lucas. Sarah Hall as the Old Countess. Only Lilo was missing. As everyone knew, Lilo was now the biggest thing in pictures and was writing her own terms as the star of the coming movie production.

Anna Harkos appeared in several stills and Nick, studying them, found her interesting. Harkos, ten years older than Letty, had never been as beautiful. But there was a sort of dark ruined glamour about her still. And if she had only a burnt-out gleam of what Letty had possessed, it was just that battered, burnt-out quality the public seemed to want. Whether or not Harkos would get the coveted movie role was still undecided, but *Masquers* had lifted her out of a marginal career into success and stardom.

Nick walked out at last into the crowded street. He was thinking of Letty, thinking for once of the actress rather than the woman. It was clear that theatrically she had belonged to another era. Even her wickedest ladies had given a sense of joy to the audience. Joy had little place in a theater celebrating with such gusto the downfall of man. The "tigress" was, after all, a dated tigress—far too innocent, far too hopelessly romantic to compete with the brutal power of a Lilo, the tortured mask of an Anna Harkos.

And yet, ironically, Letty was more famous now than she had ever been. She had come triumphantly back into style by the simple expedient of dying. For a bewildered public, accepting their new, angry theater, still longed in its heart for the old. "Remembering Letty" was taking on the intensity of a cult. Cinema houses were coining money with her old movies. Giant posters of the beautiful face gazed out of shopwindows in Greenwich Village. One even began to hear rumors of a "definitive biography," a book that would rake every wound life had made in her screaming flesh. For gaping wounds and screaming flesh were also part of the new, strange style. Not a week passed that some magazine did not serve it all up again: the suicide of the husband, the freak death of Stramm, the son arrested on a murder charge, the climactic collapse on opening night and, of course, the Last Great Romance—the handsome and mysterious sculptor in whose arms she had grandly died.

Nick had learned to take it without flinching, to tell his friends with an ironic laugh, that atrocious as it all was, it had boosted his sales. And, in fact, he was selling better than he had in years. A Texas millionaire with a taste for the macabre had even bought *Empyrean*. The so-called "Death Sculpture," dragged out of Santini's warehouse, now pointed to its heaven somewhere in the vaster limbo of a Texas ranch.

More than a year had passed since the deaths of Kenneth Stramm and Ralph Jackman took up space in the daily press. The flurry of interest when the case against Keith Tilden was dropped had also had its day. In the course of that time more earthshaking headlines had appeared. Whole populations in Southeast Asia had been bombed out of existence. Students were shot down on the campuses of American universities. And taking a slow hold in the popular mind was a stunned suspicion that gangsters and thugs were in control of the nation.

Like everyone else, Nick turned all this on and off with his television set. For people have interests of their own. In the face of world turmoil and national uproar, Nick continued to concern himself with his own problems, not the least of them his day-to-day relations with his landlord.

These, fortunately, had improved. Life, working its deft invisible magic, had quietly mended the rift. Without words or explanations, a measure of peace had come back to the gray brick house on Washington Street.

Arriving at his studio one afternoon, Nick found his water taps had run dry. He went up to the parlor floor to inquire and was told there that Bacchus was talking to visitors in the upstairs studio. Nick accordingly took the automatic elevator and rode up to the top floor.

A group of three were gathered there, all chatting and having drinks before a pleasantly blazing fire. Midge sent him friendship with ecstatic blown kisses. Arnaboldi's smile referred to old quarrels even as it charmingly erased them. And Bacchus, standing by the fireplace, called genially, "Hello there, Nick! Come in and have a drink with us!"

160

The subject of water taps dealt with and dismissed, Nick settled down to talk awhile. All the same, the little group around the fireplace had given him a momentary catch at the throat. Bacchus. Midge. Arnaboldi. All three had been in the house on the night Kenneth Stramm had died! Nick counted off the others in his mind. Keith. Bettina. Jackman. Letty. Seven then, besides Stramm. And out of that seven, one of them—

Listening with half an ear to the theatrical gossip around the fireplace, Nick was once again obsessed. The riddle. He was never free of it. Which one? Which of the seven?

The logical suspect, he mused, was Keith. Keith had lied about the Two Dakotas. He had vanished when he knew Nick wanted an explanation. He was a young man given to sullen moods and violent explosions of temper. One could easily imagine him smoldering over some old hatred, and according to Bettina, he had bitterly resented Stramm for years.

Balancing all this, of course, was Letty's confession in the hospital. Yet Midge had denied that the confession was true. As time passed, Nick found himself less and less able to believe it. There was no way in or out of the web. For the thousandth time he tried to put it out of his mind and forget it.

He came out of these thoughts, aware that Arnaboldi was addressing him. "I've some news, Nick," he was saying. "I've just been telling these people here that Keith and Bettina are going to be married."

Nick said it was decent of the young people to have waited so long.

"More than a year!" Arnaboldi sighed. "Now they will marry, the kids."

Midge said something vague about the draft. Bacchus grunted out that marrying Bettina would not keep Keith out of the army.

"Well, he won't go overseas," Arnaboldi rejoined. "These young people would rather leave the country than take part in the war. I believe Keith and Bettina will settle in Canada if he is called up."

Midge sipped her drink. "How is Keith, anyway?" she asked Arnaboldi. "I had no idea you were seeing him."

"I've seen very little of him. But he did call to tell me about the wedding." After hesitating, Arnaboldi said, "The fact is, Keith would like us all to come. To the wedding, you know. Nick too. Nick especially, in fact."

"I would certainly think Nick especially!" Bacchus coldly remarked. "Since Nick happens to have saved his life!" He turned to him. "Did he ever call and thank you for it?"

Nick said, "He sent a flyer about his exhibit. But something came up and I wasn't able to go."

Arnaboldi said hesitantly, "Well, he's getting married. I thought we might drop in to wish him luck." He looked hopefully at the others.

"I can't do that," Midge said. She was upset. "Keith shouldn't ask me to do it!" she burst out again. "Please don't think I'm cruel or vindictive. I know Keith didn't mean for that gun to go off. But it did go off, and Ralph is gone—" She searched for a handkerchief, her eyes flooding. "He's Letty's son," she tearfully acknowledged. "I do wish him luck. You all know that!"

"Well, I most emphatically wish him nothing of the kind!" Bacchus wrathfully declared. "I will most certainly *not* be at his wedding! I took that boy in. I gave him a home when his own house had become intolerable to him. I was a friend, and I proved it. But I am no longer a friend. He put us all through a living hell. He walked away scot-free while *we* paid the price for his monstrous anger, his monstrous malice!" He stopped short as Midge and Arnaboldi both uttered a sharp warning. He had said more than was wise, and they all looked at Nick apprehensively.

"It's all right," Nick assured them in a tired way. "I know there was a fight between Keith and Stramm that night. I've guessed for a long time that—well, that Keith must have done it."

He had brought it out into the open. A long moment ticked by. Bacchus said, "I didn't exactly mean for you to get that idea, Nick. In point of fact—he didn't."

"Then who?" Nick cried sharply, involuntarily. "It was one of you? Who? Which one?"

After a curious silence, Arnaboldi said with a grave face, "I think Nick has a right to an answer."

"I'm perfectly willing to let him have the facts," Bacchus rapped out. "In my opinion he should have had them a long time back. But I can't act alone in this matter." He looked at Midge.

"Well, Midge, what do you say?" Arnaboldi asked. His eyes were sad. "Letty and Ralph are both gone. What difference does it make now?"

"None. None." She gave up with a kind of despair, her golden head bowed. "Nick was with her to the last. He has a right to know."

"Well?" Bacchus put it to him. "Shall we speak? You may like it better if we don't."

Nick sat very still. From head to foot his whole body was tingling. The answer was quivering all around him. It was in the very air of this room.

"Well?" Bacchus challenged.

Nick wavered, but the old compulsion was there. To know. Finally to know. "I want the truth," he said. "Whatever it is."

"I daresay you can take it," Bacchus calmly replied.

And seating himself near the fire, he began.

"None of us wanted Letty to marry Kenneth Stramm," Bacchus said. "We all knew she was making a bad mistake. But Stramm had worn her down, the date was set and we had to accept it."

"We hoped for the best," Arnaboldi put in mournfully.

Midge broke in with a touch of old anger. "He wanted control of her career, and he wanted control of her money! And he would have gotten it too!"

"Well, there was absolutely no way we could prevent it," Bacchus said, taking up the thread. "As Arnaboldi says, we hoped for the best." He waited a moment and went on. "Letty had taken a place on Long Island that summer, Keith was also there. Apparently the summer went badly. Keith and Stramm had never gotten along and with the wedding getting closer tensions were probably worse than usual. There was a series of collisions capped by a bad blowup. It was about some nonsense, I daresay, but Keith walked out. He came to me, asked if he could sleep in the spare bedroom until he found a place of his

163

own. Naturally I told him he could stay as long as he liked. But of course Letty was extremely upset. She didn't want to marry while Stramm and Keith were on the outs. That was why I gave the party. I thought it would bring the two of them together."

Bacchus sighed heavily, stared fixedly at the floor and then went on. "Kenneth was not a bad man, Nick. He was just a deeply unhappy and untalented man. Nobody liked him. He was vain and weak and spiteful. But he had his good points. He did love Letty, and he came that night, I am sure, with the best of intentions."

Midge interrupted to say that Keith too had been willing to make friends and be reconciled.

"Apparently they were both willing to make the effort," Bacchus said, "yet it didn't come off. I suppose the situation was too touchy. Stramm was always impossible, and that night he was even more so. He felt that Letty had put him on trial and that everything now depended on his pleasing Keith. It humiliated him. He was very insecure, you know. I don't think he was sure even then that Letty would go through with it and marry him. So it was rough sledding from the start. That was why I asked Keith to get out the I Ching. I thought it might loosen everyone up, amuse them, make them relax a bit."

"And it *was* amusing, the magic book," Arnaboldi said, remembering it.

Midge took up the story. "It was Letty who asked the first question. She asked about the play."

"Yes, the play!" Arnaboldi was vividly recalling it. "Bettina read out the answer. It was fantastic. The play was going to be a smash, and we were all going to get rich! We were excited as hell, laughing—we were just like children!"

"And tactless as children!" Bacchus unexpectedly growled. "We should have realized what it was doing to Stramm. How could he take it when his own play had been such a total ghastly failure!"

"Aie! Poor Kenneth!" Arnaboldi saw it all now. "That was why he lashed out the way he did."

"Of course. He had to prove the book was a hoax."

164

"Didn't he ask some nasty question?" Midge frowned. "Something about a horse?"

"A horse? Wasn't it a joke of some kind?"

"It was a question about Keith and Bettina."

"Well, he insisted on asking *something*. Keith finally gave in and threw the coins. That's when we got that queer message." Midge shuddered. "Stramm was in danger, the book said. Terrible danger."

"And that other queer bit," Arnaboldi reminded her in a low voice. "The bit about the crevice."

"It made no sense at the time."

"None at all. Stramm had proved the book was a hoax." Arnaboldi paused. "But somehow the fun went out of things after that."

"Oh, the party was a bust," Bacchus said. "Everyone knew by then that it was hopeless. Midge and I made some fresh drinks, but it was no use. People were simply waiting for the moment they could go home."

"Why didn't we?" Arnaboldi asked with a kind of anguish. "Why didn't we all go?"

"Well, we didn't. We stood around waiting while Stramm and Keith got into some dreary wrangle about the New Left and the counterculture."

"Oh, yes, it was always the New Left and the counterculture!" Midge laughed scornfully. "Nobody was listening. We were bored to death with it. We just wanted to leave."

That was the way Nick heard the story—with each of them cutting in on the other to explain, to correct, to add some forgotten detail. From time to time one of them got to his feet, showing Nick where someone had been standing, what someone else had been doing. And Nick, watching, listening, began to feel time itself was rolling back, began to feel that the events they described were unfolding before him, as they had unfolded that night.

165

K'an
The Abyss

The danger can no longer be averted.
Nothing can save him.

The guests had lingered, against their will, while Stramm put his question to the magic book. But the answer, when it came, was just a queer rigamarole. Something about an abyss, a crevice—it made no sense at all. Even Keith could not explain it.

By this time the party was not so much breaking up as simply coming apart. Midge had mislaid one of her gloves. Dr. Jackman was searching for it among the sofa cushions. Bacchus brought in the coats and wraps and stood, impassive, waiting for his guests to depart. And Letty, impatient and tired, called to Stramm that she wanted to go.

Stramm, however, could not seem to tear himself away from his wrangle with Keith. He remained where he was, jockeying for the last word.

The magic book was a dud, and Stramm had proved it. Flushed with one victory, he wanted another. How did all this magic and tossing of coins fit in with the program of the New Left, he asked again. And did Keith mean to bring down capitalism by means of soothsaying, incantations and voodoo?

"We won't need any voodoo," Keith said. He added defiantly, "When the time comes, the working class will be on the side of the revolution."

"But whatever makes you think so, Keith?" Stramm demanded in his offensive superior way. "Why on earth should the working class join your doomed little revolution?"

On the other side of the room a general atmosphere of exhaustion and disarray was taking over. Jackman found his wife's glove. Bacchus helped Letty into her wrap. The guests were simply preparing to go. The argument between Keith and Stramm about the New Left was too old a story. No one bothered to listen until it suddenly took a new and jarring turn.

This began with Stramm insisting in his nagging way that Keith and his friends had never worked a day in their lives. To which Keith returned gratingly, "And when did you do *your* last day's hard labor, Kenneth?"

"I've worked," Stramm said. "I've paid my way. Can you say as much? You've never done anything but live off your father's money."

Everyone heard that. The room had gone very still.

After a short pause, Keith said pleasantly, "And now you think it's time *you* lived off my father's money. Right, Kenneth?"

By now everyone was riveted. Letty called in a high sharp voice that both men were to end their discussion. When neither of them answered, she swept down between them, wild flashes in her eyes. "That's enough!" she flared. "Stop it, both of you!" She turned on Stramm. "You promised me this wouldn't happen. I'm warning you, Kenneth! I'm warning you for the last time!"

"And I've had enough of your warnings," Kenneth suddenly shrieked. The whole tone of his skin had turned dark and livid. "If you want to back out, go ahead! Back out!"

Letty, absolutely furious, cried, "I have already backed out!"

Whether she meant it or not, her words came as a horrible shock to Stramm. He fell back, seemed to strangle, and finally gasped out, "Fine! Then this is the end. The end of everything. I'll go!" He began struggling into his coat. "I'll go," he repeated wildly. "Keith has always wanted this. Now he's had his way!"

Letty denied this with disgust, but she was cut short by Keith who said, in an unanswerable tone, that he would speak for himself. Although this was addressed to his mother, his eyes never left those of Stramm. There was something hypnotic about the way these two never took their eyes off each other.

"So you've come out with it at last, have you?" Stramm jeered. "It's no news to me that you've hated me. I've known that for years."

"If I did, I had my reasons," Keith returned.

"I tried to make something of you," Stramm went on. His voice cracked. He was crying, the tears rolling down his cheeks. "I did my best. It was never any use. You hated me from the start. The money. You were always afraid I'd get my hands on the money. That's why you hated me."

"I hated you," Keith said steadily, "but not because of the money."

"Well, you've had your way," Stramm said. "You've succeeded. You'll never see me again."

But though he made his farewells, Stramm could not seem to go. One idea obsessed and held him there—that Keith had always had his way. He made quite a speech about it. It was Letty, it appeared, who from the start had given Keith his way. She had encouraged Keith's friendships with dangerous radicals. She had shut her eyes to his trafficking in drugs. She had raised him to be a great artist when everyone knew he had absolutely no talent.

"Shut *up!*" Letty cried, trying to shout him down. "Shut up, you utter damned *fool!*"

But nothing could stop Stramm in his headlong rush to his

own destruction. Having committed the outrageous, he now added the unforgivable—his cruel, senseless attack on Bettina. Letty, he said, had allowed Keith to become involved with a girl who was a mental case and a misfit.

Alarmed voices on every side were now calling on Stramm to be silent. He only shouted the louder. "Look at her!" He pointed. "Look at her eyes! She's been in an institution! Can't you see it? Are you all blind?"

Bettina turned deathly white and, with a choked exclamation, ran out of the room. Keith, calling her name, rushed out after her. Letty, devastated and in tears, sank into a chair and told Stramm the wedding was off.

"You never meant to go through with it!" he threw back bitterly. "You and your son have both always loathed and despised me!" He stood there weeping in his coat. And indeed he had reason. For he had never truly hated Keith and had smarted all these years only because he could not win his love.

While a general sense of helplessness and collapse took over inside the house, Keith and Bettina were carrying the drama out into the street. Keith caught the girl just outside the door. It was here that Bettina made to Keith her pitiful confession of past mental illness.

Stramm's attack had left Bettina all but dead. She renounced all rights to Keith, renounced all hope, and proclaimed herself unfit for Keith or any other man. She was gripped by a fear that her illness was not over, that it would and must return.

Keith heard her out in an agony of love for her and an agony of hate for the man who had just caused her such harm. In a violent upsurge of both emotions, he went back into the house with one idea in his mind—revenge.

The guests, already sufficiently unnerved, were totally unprepared for his sudden reappearance. The sound of running footsteps in the hall, followed by Keith himself, startled all of them out of their wits. He had stopped only to get the gun out of Bacchus's bedroom. He came in, waving it in the air and shouting, "Out of my way, all of you! He's done all the harm he's going to do. Now he's going to learn his lesson!"

Bettina trailed in behind him, whimpering. She was begging

him not to do violence, but he was much too set on avenging her to hear anything she said.

The sight of the gun sent everyone scattering in a mindless panic. Stramm, horribly frightened, ran half across the room before he remembered his dignity. He stopped and commanded Keith to drop the gun, but this try at authority was betrayed by a pitifully croaking voice and a face entirely drained of blood.

Keith spoke again, grimly, "Stand clear, all of you. This is the man who killed my father. He's going to pay for it now."

At these words an icy chill came over everyone. Nobody, even in the first momentary panic, had believed Keith would actually use that gun. Now, what had seemed impossible and even absurd, seemed less so. A chorus of voices rang out, telling Keith he was making a mistake, that he was wrong, utterly wrong.

"He's crazy!" Stramm looked right and left, appealing to everyone. "I wasn't even there. I was *here* when Tilden shot himself. I was here in New York!"

Letty's voice, more angry than frightened, rang out over the others. "Keith, this is insane! Kenneth had nothing to do with it. Nothing, I tell you!"

"Oh, he didn't pull the trigger!" Keith was full of scorn. "He didn't have guts enough for that. But he killed him just the same. I know what he did. I heard. I've known for years why my father killed himself, and now he's going to pay for it!"

Stramm made a quick run along the wall. "I told him I was her lover," he panted out. "It was the truth. It's not my fault he couldn't take it." Going into a blind panic, he threw both hands over his face and screamed, "Do you think I'm the only one she was sleeping with?"

That was a bad mistake, for then and there, Keith fired. Over the report of the revolver, a twanging sound was heard. The aluminum sculpture near the window began violently bobbing and rotating. A number of metal disks fell off it. The bullet had passed through the central disk and buried itself in the wall.

Chaos followed. Jackman ran for the door and stood looking back with his eyes rolling in his head. Bettina was screaming. Bacchus sprang on Keith from behind and grappled with him for the gun. Letty rushed between Keith and Stramm, shielding

Stramm with her body and shouting furiously at Keith to give up the gun.

"Get her away!" Keith screamed. "I'll kill her too! I'll kill the two of them!" Exerting all his strength, he threw Bacchus off and raised the gun on a trembling arm. Midge and Arnaboldi, terrified, dragged Letty away and held her forcibly. "Run!" Letty sobbed out to Stramm. "Run, damn you! Don't you see he's going to shoot?"

Either Stramm was paralyzed by fear, or he had determined to save a remnant of his manhood before Letty. With the gun directly on him, he did not move.

He had come to a crouching halt before the window—that open yawning window with its terrible low sill. That was when the tragedy took place. For Letty did something now that nobody could have foreseen. Tearing free of Midge and Arnaboldi, she ran with the full force of her body against Stramm—and pushed him out.

Stramm lost his footing, tried to right himself, caught vainly at the window handles and fell screaming—a scream that was abruptly cut short. Nobody could believe it had happened. One moment Stramm was in the room; the next there was nobody at the window but Letty.

What followed was the queer, rolling, pitching silence of a plane when the motor goes off. In that totally suspended moment Letty, sobbing a little, turned to her son and said, "Now you don't have to kill him, Keith. I did it for you."

At this point in his story Bacchus got up and poked at the ashes in the fireplace, sending up a faint stream of sparks. A heavy silence had fallen over the room.

"So it was Letty," Nick said at last very low.

"She had to!" Arnaboldi answered. "There was no other way to save Keith."

"Save him?"

Arnaboldi said firmly, "From being a murderer!"

"I always said she had no motive," Nick muttered in a dazed voice. "But she had one after all."

"Trust Letty to think of a new one!" Bacchus growled.

Nick got up, walked to the window and stood looking out over the rooftops. He turned back after a time and said quietly, "Then you were all in on it!"

"All." Bacchus assented. "We were all here when it happened and all in the same great danger."

"We would have gone to pieces, I think," Arnaboldi said, "if not for Bacchus. He was the only one who kept his head, who made us see we had to have a plan."

"Oh, a plan was imperative," Bacchus coolly declared. "First off, there was Stramm himself. It was quite possible he was not dead at all. He might have been lying down there, unconscious, maybe, crippled for life, maybe, but alive! We had to find out about that. Being a doctor, poor Jackman had to go down and see whether anything could still be done. Keith went with him to give him courage. They came back soon enough. Bringing with them the ghastly facts."

"They told you Stramm was wedged into—?"

"Exactly." Bacchus had to take a breath, remembering it. "Things were pretty bad after that. Letty went completely to pieces. She kept screaming, 'The book! The book told us!' She was in a state of near insanity and horror because of that damned book. She wanted us to call the police so she could give herself up. We didn't know how in hell to handle her, three of us had to drag her away from the telephone. Jackman found a sedative and somehow got it into her. And Keith swore if she gave herself up he would confess his own part in the affair—the gun, the attempted shooting and so forth. After that Letty just collapsed. She went into a semi-torpid state and agreed to everything."

Nick said, "So you laid out your plans."

"We laid out our plans. The aluminum sculpture was to be hidden in the basement. The bullet hole was to be covered up and concealed. Everyone was to go home as if nothing had occurred. And you, Nick, were to discover the body when you came home." Bacchus paused in his story long enough to say, "I hope you will forgive us someday for that."

"Then the scene out in the court really was staged for me," Nick said thoughtfully.

"Oh, yes. You were absolutely right about that. It was Keith who went down again and turned on the illumination. If we had left the court in darkness you would have seen nothing until you woke next morning. Keith and I couldn't wait out the night knowing all the time that Kenneth was in the court."

"It was an enormous risk you all took," Nick commented.

"Well, we wanted to save her if we could," Bacchus said simply. "We all loved her, you know."

"We were her friends," Arnaboldi quietly and sadly added.

"The weak link was Jackman," Bacchus went on. "We thought Midge could control him. It was our greatest mistake. He was under too much pressure, and the I Ching hexagram sent him over the edge. I think we should tell you, Nick"—he turned to him—"that Keith knew nothing about that anonymous message. It was Bettina who sent it."

"The anonymous threat? *Bettina?*"

"But, you see, it wasn't a threat," said Arnaboldi.

"Bettina was afraid," Midge said. "She knew Ralph was talking too much—telling too much."

Bacchus explained. "Being frightened, Bettina consulted the I Ching. That's what she always does. About everything. As bad luck would have it, she got that damnable message about the Abyss. She sent it to Jackman to tell him he was courting danger. In her rather childish way, she thought she was helping him."

"Bettina lives by the I Ching," Midge said, shaking her head over it mournfully.

"These young people do," Arnaboldi affirmed.

"She will doubtless regret it the rest of her life," Bacchus said, "but it was poor Ralph who paid the price."

A silence fell.

"That part of it was my fault," Midge said quietly. "I asked too much of Ralph. But I thought it only right to try to save Letty. No matter what anyone may say"—her head went up—"I have never for a moment believed she meant to push him out."

Bacchus weighed the idea. "She may have simply wanted to get Stramm out of gun range," he conceded, "since he himself could not seem to move."

"I must admit I've never been sure about Keith either," Arnaboldi suddenly declared. "It seems to me he meant to humiliate and frighten Stramm but not to kill him. That first gunshot—the one that went into the wall—I've always thought the gun may have gone off by itself. Keith looked as startled as anyone when it happened."

"Nonsense, Leo! Absolute nonsense!" Bacchus turned quite red with anger. "Keith has taken you in. Completely. I'm sorry to say it, but he is a vicious young man. He was the cause of Stramm's death, the cause of Ralph's death—"

"Bill! Bill! Ralph was an accident!"

"He died just the same." Bacchus was past reason. "Don't tell me about Keith. He killed Stramm sure as if he'd done the pushing. He never went to see Letty, never even called her. He broke her heart, and as far as I'm concerned he killed her too."

Midge and Arnaboldi both felt this was unfair. Bacchus would not budge. He insisted Keith had killed Letty with his neglect. Nick remained silent. He had views of his own about who had killed Letty.

"As you see, we have come to no agreement about all this," Bacchus finally said to Nick with a sigh. "Still, we've given you as much as we know ourselves. We can't do more than that."

Nick was lost in thought.

"I've always understood," he said, taking it up one last time, "that the party split up that night. Bacchus and Midge went into the bar, while the rest of you stayed in the living room. At a certain point Stramm walked out and climbed up to the top floor." Nick looked around him. "Climbed up here, in fact, where the tragedy took place. Well, ever since that night I have asked myself two questions. What made Stramm leave the living room and go up to the top floor. And who came up here with him." Nick looked around from face to face. "Now the story seems to be," he continued slowly, "that *all* of you were up here with him. From what you tell me, Bacchus and Keith were grappling for the gun, Jackman ran to the door, Bettina was screaming . . . did *everyone* follow Stramm up those stairs?"

After a curious beat of time Bacchus cried out to Nick, "Why do you ask? We've already given you the answer!"

And indeed, Nick, silent and shaken, felt it was closer than ever before.

One last time the familiar memory picture emerged. It was five in the morning. He was standing out on Washington Street, looking up at the windows of the house. There was something he *knew*, something quite simple. And this time, as he groped for it, the last piece moved quietly into place.

For it was to those *topmost* windows he had raised his eyes that morning. It was up there he had searched, wanting to make sure the lights were out, the party really over. . . .

He had it now and wondered why it had escaped him so long. For it had never seemed right that Bacchus would entertain his most intimate friends in those cold, formal rooms on the parlor floor.

"It was staring at me all the time," he said slowly, looking again from face to face. "Stramm never left the living room at all that night."

"He never was *in* the living room," Bacchus said.

"Yes, I see it now," Nick responded. "That business about the living room—the bar—"

"An invention. A blind." Bacchus confessed it with a tired smile. "We were up here, Nick. All of us. This is where the party was that night. The whole thing, from beginning to end. But you've always really known that, haven't you?"

And just under the conscious level, Nick always had.

The Power of the Great

(The Oracle Speaks
for the Last Time)

*That which is strong
and that which is right are one.
The road has opened.*

As Nick later recalled it, everything about that particular afternoon with Edwin Grey was just a trifle odd. Even the light slanting in through the blinds seemed to play tricks that day. The long rays of the setting sun fell so intensely across one side of the sparely furnished room as to plunge the other half into a queer colorless shadow. In this uncertain light Grey's outline seemed at times to waver and fade. There were moments when Nick could barely make out his friend in the dusk; he seemed no more than a disembodied mind, a creature unsubstantial as one of his own equations.

176

It was perhaps this fanciful notion that made it possible for Nick to reveal a great many secrets that day. It took time, but he finally got through it all—the long chain of events that had followed Stramm's death, a chain that ended in the recent revelations of Nick's three friends in Washington Street.

Grey heard him out, interrupting only with a question or two that showed how intently he listened. As usual he seemed to make no judgments and to feel no surprise. And when it was over, the voice coming from the shadow was pleasant and ordinary as ever. "Your friends seem to have left you with more of a puzzle than an answer" was Grey's calm comment. "Did the lady intend to push him out? Did the son intend to shoot? All that still seems to be very much up in the air."

Nick admitted this was so. "Everyone was there," he said. "None of them agree on what really happened."

"Well, what do you think yourself?" Grey expanded on it. "Did either of them mean to kill the man? Was the whole thing perhaps a tragic accident, a tragic misunderstanding?"

Nick took some time before he replied. "Keith may or may not have intended to shoot. For me that's of secondary importance. The point is that Letty thought he would! She had to act, and there was no time. Since she could not save Stramm, she saved Keith. My feeling is that she acted deliberately."

"You seem almost to suggest she was right," Grey murmured.

"No, I don't say that." Nick frowned, wanting to make himself clear. "You see, throughout the whole business, I was afraid of one thing—that Letty was really somebody else, somebody I didn't know at all. When I found her with a gun in her hand, the world rocked. If she had killed, killed in cold blood to protect her interests, then I didn't know her—had never known her. She had worn a mask with me, and I was a fool to have trusted her."

"The question then of right and wrong—?"

"It simply doesn't concern me," Nick asserted with some impatience. "What she did—the reason she did it, the impulsiveness of it, the *recklessness* of it—don't you see? There was no other woman, no mask. It was Letty. It was the way she would act."

Grey said calmly, "Well, you seem to have cared about her quite extraordinarily. I am amazed, Nick, at how much you did for her."

"Oh, everyone talks about how much I did for her," Nick said in a tired way. "Maybe I loved her. I suppose I did. I can't see that it matters much. It didn't help her any." He waved off what Grey was about to say. "I know. I drove her out there and the rest of it. All that was useless. It was Keith she cared about. All those wild moves she made, all her lies, mistakes—everything was for Keith. And I didn't care a damn about Keith. I was annoyed he was so much in the picture. I wanted her as my mistress. As a mother she bored me. I made that plain enough."

"You should try to forget it," Grey told him gently.

"Oh, I'll forget it," Nick assured him lightly. "I forget it more and more each day. Pretty soon I won't remember it at all." He brooded. "Circumstances were pretty black against her. I don't blame myself as much as I did. Only there are things I wish—" He broke off.

"They may not be as bad as you think, Nick."

"Maybe not." He shrugged. "I threw it in her face that night that she was an actress—said I didn't want any of her acting. I wish I hadn't done that. It hurt her, and it was a rotten thing to say. Of all the women I've known, Letty was the realest."

Grey let a moment go by and took it up again at another point. "What about the young man? The son. What's happened to him?"

"Keith? He's all right. In fact, he's going to be married." Nick added that he had been invited to the wedding. "I may have to go, too," he remarked ruefully, "since Bacchus and Midge have backed out of it."

"Why shouldn't you all go? Do you blame this young man for what happened?"

"I do blame him," Nick admitted. "But in a way I'm sorry for him, too. He'll be carrying a burden the rest of his life. It must be hard on a man to think he's Che Guevara, and then find out that all the time he was only—"

"Only Hamlet?"

Nick smiled at the aptness of it. "That's who they say we all are." He thought about things, not very happily. "I suppose it would be nice if someone were there for Keith. Maybe Arnaboldi can carry the day."

"If you feel that way about it, why not go?"

Nick answered slowly. "Because Keith wants me to be his friend. He wants me to be part of his life. And I don't want to give him false hopes."

Grey shrugged. "In that case you can always be out of town."

"Yes, I must find some excuse," Nick absently agreed. But he was deep in his own thoughts. "These angry activist kids have dominated the scene for a decade now," he said. "I've never seen a generation quite like it. But I wonder where they'll be in another ten years, say, when the excitement is over and we've all gone back to normal again."

"Oh, I doubt very much we're ever going to do that," Grey remarked quietly. "That's gone, Nick."

"Gone for good, eh?" He grimaced a little over the wreck of a world he remembered—put it away with everything else he had lost. "The kids are making a last try for us, I suppose," he finally said. "You've got to hand it to them. They're standing up against the war, standing up for justice, putting themselves on the line. It's more than we're doing. I admire them, but there's just no common ground. I don't understand the drugs. I don't fathom their politics. I don't care much for their art. Keith is twenty. I'm twice that. The tragic view of life is all right, I suppose, but it happens to bore me. I simply don't care to get involved."

He had ended harshly, almost with anger, and Grey looked at him, surprised. "You don't have to go to this wedding," he remarked.

"I don't intend to!" Nick returned. But he turned away, muttering, "I'm damned if I know what to do."

It was somewhere at this point that Edwin Grey brought up the I Ching. Nick thought he was joking. "I wouldn't dare!" was his wry response. "That book of yours predicts only calamities, Edwin. And they all come true!"

"Well, the bad can't endure forever," Grey said. "It's time for

179

the wheel to turn." And rising, he turned on the lamps, for it had grown quite dark by now.

In this warmer, steadier light the last of Nick's odd fancy dissolved. Grey was no longer a voice coming out of a grayish dusk but a man of flesh, bone, muscle, and nerve, a man fallible as himself. Indeed, Grey was more fallible since, unlike Nick, he believed in powers other than human.

Apparently he was quite in earnest about the I Ching, for he took it off its shelf and placed it on the table. Nick did nothing to stop him. He was so troubled these days he was ready to accept help from any source at all—even this one. But it was the last time Nick would ever consult the *Book of Changes*, for never at any point in his life did he really believe in it.

Grey placed three coins on the table and waited for Nick to decide on his question.

"I suppose I could ask the big one," Nick said.

"The big one?"

"You said yourself it was all still a puzzle. Did Keith mean to shoot Stramm? Did Letty mean to push him out? Which of them was truly guilty? Letty? Keith? Both?"

Grey found the query interesting, but Nick changed his mind at the last moment and withdrew it. "She wanted to be the guilty one," he said. "Maybe we should let it stay that way."

"What about the wedding?"

Nick considered it, but without great interest. "Why disturb an ancient Chinese gentleman for anything so trivial? How to refuse an unwanted invitation. A point of etiquette."

"Well"—Grey smiled—"who better than the Chinese on a point of etiquette?"

"I guess I could give it a try." Nick reflected and said, "Here it is then. Isn't it best not to raise false hopes by accepting the invitation? Won't I be hurting Keith more in the long run? Isn't honesty in such matters always best?"

"Is that one question?"

Nick replied briskly, "It is!"

Grey tossed his coins, drawing up his lines as he did so.

Turning pages, he read aloud from the text of the fifty-sixth hexagram:

"'Fire on the mountain—the symbol of the Wanderer. The Wanderer has no home and must rely on the goodwill of strangers. He must be circumspect and careful in his behavior, for he is without friends. Although he may obtain gold enough to pay his food and lodgement, the heart of the Wanderer is without joy. When he is alone, he weeps and laments.'"

"Is that all?" Nick looked blank.

"It seems so—since there is no moving line."

"Do you see any connection?" Nick obviously did not.

"It does seem rather oblique." Grey studied the page. "The Wanderer may perhaps refer to this Keith Tilden, a young man with money but no friends."

Nick was struck. "Keith may soon really be a wanderer," he told Grey. "He may decide to leave the country rather than go into the army."

Grey, intent on the page, tried a second interpretation. "The message may also mean that your absence at his wedding makes this young man feel homeless—as though he were a wanderer."

"Well, I don't know," Nick suddenly argued. "I'm homeless myself. I've got my work, but I've got nothing else. I think *I'm* the wanderer!"

"Well"—Grey stirred unhappily—"it may also refer to you."

"Not a very cheerful idea," Nick muttered.

Grey admitted it was not.

A bleak little silence fell.

Suddenly, for some reason, Nick came out of his dejected state. Getting to his feet he snapped his fingers several times, shut both eyes tight, and exclaimed in a strong voice full of animation, "Throw the coins again, Edwin! We're going to ask it the other way round!"

Grey swept the coins up again. He did not understand but had caught Nick's excitement.

"Hold it a bit!" Nick was concentrating hard, eyes still shut. "Here's the way we ask it this time. Shall I go to the wedding?

181

Shall I be with Keith that day? Because it will mean something to him to have me there—because I'm the only link he has now with his mother—because he was Letty's son and maybe he should have been my son too?"

"Is that all of it?" Grey was blinking.

"What in hell more can I put into it?"

Grey threw the coins six times and drew up his symbol.

"Well?" Nick asked impatiently. "Is it good or bad?"

Grey seemed a bit overwhelmed. "It's good, Nick. Quite good, in fact."

"Then let's hear it."

The message, from the thirty-fourth hexagram, read as follows:

"The sky among the mountain peaks—The Power of the Great. Strength, magnanimity, courage, truth. Every day he renews his bright virtue. . . ."

Nick gave a shout of laughter. "All that? All because I'm going to a funny little wedding in the East Village?" But his whole face had cleared. He even looked younger.

"You have received a moving line at the top," Grey informed him. "This gives us, of course, a second hexagram. So we will now learn where your present course is tending."

"This is where it all goes downhill again!" Nick exclaimed. He was in high good humor. "Let's have it. I'm ready for the worst!"

Grey changed the straight line at the top to a broken line, drew up the new hexagram accordingly, and turned pages for the message.

"Let's have it!" Nick repeated, laughing. "Whatever it is!"

"Come and see for yourself."

Walking around, Nick glanced down over Grey's shoulder. The book lay open at "T'ai"—the eleventh hexagram. The English title at the head of the page was PEACE.

"That's not a bad word," Nick said.

"No better in any book."

They read the text together:

"Peace. The way of the mean departs. The way of the great approaches. Heaven and earth unite to prepare a new beginning.

High and low mingle and are of one will. All feuds are at an end. Great good fortune and success."

"Peace." Nick mused on it a while longer. "Is there really a road that leads to that, Edwin?"

"The I Ching says you're on it."

"But does anyone ever *get* there?"

"I don't know." Grey had his own ruefulness. "I guess you have to stay on the road, Nick. You can't swerve."

"That's the part that's hard," Nick said.

"But worth it," said Grey, "to get there."

And smiling pleasantly at his longtime friend, he quietly closed the book.

AUTHOR'S NOTE

I have used several versions of the I Ching in this book, taking some texts from the standard Bollingen edition, others from the translations of John Blofeld or James Legge. In the interest of brevity some of the texts have been slightly altered.